Surf's Up

TWO NOVELLAS

A Tide Worth Turning

Message in a Bottle

A Tide Worth Turning/Message In A Bottle
(2 in One Volume)

Copyright 2016 Beth Wiseman
Published by Beth Wiseman in Fayetteville, Texas

Cover design: Beth Wiseman
Interior design: Caitlin Greer

ISBN-13: 978-0-9976610-2-6

A Tide Worth Turning

A NOVELLA

BETH WISEMAN

To Jamie Foley

Chapter One

Addison paced across her mother's living room as sweat dampened her temples and the base of her neck. May was already punishing them with Texas temperatures that were usually reserved for July and August. But Lee Ann Burke had a steadfast rule not to run the air conditioning until July. If there was any saving grace at all, it was the ocean pushing a breeze ashore, which wafted through the screened windows of the house Addison had grown up in. She breathed in the briny aroma, a smell she'd haul to her grave someday, with enough good and bad memories to keep her balanced on the plank she'd been walking since her father died.

She glanced at her smartphone, wondering if she was going to make it to her next appointment on time. The continuous drip of the kitchen faucet around the corner felt like water torture against her left temple. She rubbed the source of the irritation. "Mom, are you sure the agency said three o'clock? It's almost three thirty."

"That's what they said." Her mother didn't glance up, but kept focused on the jigsaw puzzle she was hunched over. Addison couldn't recall a time that her family—small as it was—had ever shared a meal at the dining table, except maybe Christmas and Thanksgiving. On most days, her mother had one of her puzzles spread atop the oak table, with a sweating glass of sweet tea nearby and an ashtray. There was still sweet tea within reach, but at least Mom had taken to smoking her cigarettes outside a few years ago, something she should have done when it became common knowledge that secondhand smoke was unhealthy. Addison recalled all the smoke she and her father had inhaled over the years, wondering if that might have contributed to her father's cancer diagnosis. Addison could still smell the stench of tobacco in the house. In light of recent events, she wondered if her mother would quit smoking. *Doubtful.* If she didn't quit after they found out Dad had cancer, Addison doubted she'd do it now.

Addison glanced at the TV trays in the stand next to the couch, the rust barely visible amidst the flowery design that vined up the legs and covered the tops. She couldn't help but smile. Some of her happiest moments were in this living room eating on TV trays and watching "Everybody Loves Raymond." Her father had loved that show, and sometimes Addison could almost hear her father's laughter late at night, right before she drifted off to sleep. Maybe he was sending her a message that she'd laugh again one day too.

Sighing, she walked to the window to get the full effect of the breeze, and after another twenty minutes of pacing the living room, she was glad to see a car turning in the driveway. "Mom, the caregiver from the agency is here." She turned to face her mother, who still didn't look up. "Mom, did you hear me?"

Slowly, her mother pulled her eyes up until they were locked with Addison's. "I had a stroke, Addie, I'm not deaf." Scowling, she looked back at her puzzle, then mumbled, "And I don't need a babysitter."

Addison shook her head, feeling a trickle of perspiration roll down her face. They'd had this conversation a dozen times, at least. "I know you don't need a babysitter, and this woman isn't being hired for that. She's just here for a few weeks, to make sure you don't fall again and to help around the house. Just until you get your strength back."

When her mother didn't respond, Addison wound around the coffee table and moved toward the front door, surprised to see a man standing on the other side of the screen. "Can I help you?"

"G'day. I'm Logan Northrupp. The agency sent me to…" He unfolded a piece of paper, scanned it, then looked at Addison. "This is 222 Beachfront Drive, right? I'm here to take care of Lee Ann Burke."

It took Addison a few seconds to realize he'd said "good day." It sounded like "goodie." Addison didn't say anything for a few moments, even though she heard a slight chuckle from her mother. "Uh…I guess I just assumed they were sending a woman."

Mom cleared her throat. "To assume is to make an—"

"Mother!" Addison peered over her shoulder. "Stop." Mom shrugged, and Addison turned back to the tall man still on the other side of the door. She eased the door open and stepped aside. "Sorry it's so hot in here."

"No problem." He smiled, and Addison tried to identify his accent, which made him even better looking than he already was. Wavy blond hair, parted in the middle, hung to the collar of his white golf shirt, which sported an emblem with the agency's logo. Logan looked more like a lifeguard than a caregiver, she thought as she eyed his chiseled arms, golden tan, and eyes as deep blue as the ocean. Her eyes cut to his left hand. No ring. There was a time in her life when Addison would have latched on to such beauty. But usually, when a single man pushing thirty looks this good, there is something wrong with him. A truckload of baggage, perhaps. Maybe a criminal record, although doubtful since he was hired out by an agency. Maybe he just wasn't a nice person. *Or gay.*

She motioned toward her mother at the table. "This is my mother, Lee Ann Burke." She paused. "Mom, this is Logan from the agency."

"Nice to meet you, Mrs. Burke."

Addison's mother finished fitting a piece of the puzzle, then stood up, and hobbled toward Addison and Logan on shaky legs, stopping a few feet short of Logan. "Addie believes that I have one foot in the

4

grave, but not only am I not planning to check out just yet, but I'm also not old enough to be called Mrs. Burke. Please just call me Lee Ann." Mom extended her hand to Logan, and while Addison cringed at her mother's idea of an introduction, it could have gone much worse.

"Then Lee Ann it is." He smiled again, flashing a set of pearly whites, then offered Addison the file folder he was holding. "This details my credentials, and there is also a list of duties that the agency gave me, if you'd like to look over it to make sure there isn't something else you'd like me to do during my time here."

Addison looked over the paperwork. He'd been a caregiver for almost two years. Not much experience, but then Addison's mother wasn't going to require much. Logan would be more of a babysitter, as Mom had said. Addison was worried her mother's mind had suffered, and the doctor said her likelihood of having another stroke was highest over the next couple of months. Even before the stroke, Mom often forgot to take her blood pressure meds.

"It says under the list of duties that you'll be here from ten in the morning until three in the afternoon, and that's fine. But it also says that you'll prepare a home-cooked meal each day for Mom's lunch." Addison glanced up at him. "She's shaky on her legs from a recent fall, but she can make her own lunch, a sandwich or something."

Smiling again, he said, "I'm a chef, so I just offered that on my own."

Addison chewed on her bottom lip in an effort not to propose to the guy here and now. *Baggage or not.*

"Hello, I'm right here," her mother interjected. "Had a stroke. Not deaf, remember?" She cleared her throat, raising her chin a bit. Mom was an attractive woman who didn't look her sixty-two years, which was surprising considering the smoking, lack of exercise, and two stiff whiskey sours each night. Addison held her breath as she waited for her mother to go on. "Logan, I think it would be lovely if you prepared us lunch every day, and I'd be happy to pay for anything you need in the way of groceries to do so." Mom moved slowly toward the front door, looking over her shoulder once. "You kids work out the details while I have a smoke. But I wouldn't be opposed to a sponge bath, if you'd like to put that on the agenda." She giggled as the screen slammed behind her.

Addison hung her head for a few moments before she looked back up at Logan and sighed. "She's my mother. And I love her. But she's opposed to having a babysitter, as she calls it. So, I hope she doesn't give you a hard time."

"I'm sure it will be fine." He wasn't smiling anymore, and Addison wondered if he was already planning to request a transfer from the agency.

Drip, drip, drip. She tried to ignore the sound of the faucet, the headache still pounding against her temple as she dug into her purse, pulling out a business card. "This is my cell number if you need me for anything. I suspect that if you just ignore most of what she says, this should be a pretty easy gig."

Addison grinned. "And she is quite capable of taking a bath on her own."

"I'm sure it will all be good. God plans the trip. I'm just the driver."

There ya go! Addison knew there had to be something wrong with this Adonis of a man. *He's a Holy Roller.*

And she didn't have room for God in her life these days. She'd trusted Him one too many times before.

Chapter Two

Logan cringed as he watched Addison walk to her car. *God plans the trip. I'm just the driver?* That barely made sense as a response to what Addison had said. Overkill, for sure. He wanted to seem like a responsible caregiver, someone she could trust. God was always in control, and Logan's faith had never wavered, despite the mess he was in now, but not everyone liked God shoved down their throat. He turned around when Lee Ann returned from the bathroom down the hall.

"If you'll show me where the vacuum cleaner and other supplies are, I'll start cleaning up around here." It was on the list, and Logan noticed the place could use an overhaul. Sand crunched beneath his loafers with every step he took, and as the midmorning sun cast rays on the hutch against the wall, he could see a thick layer of dust coating the top. It smelled musty too.

Lee Ann frowned. "I just cleaned this morning before you and Addison got here." She eased herself into a tan recliner and pointed to the couch. "Let's chat."

Logan glanced around again, wondering exactly what she'd cleaned and if she should even be attempting that. The woman was wobbly on her feet. "Um...okay." He looked at his watch before sitting down on the couch. A gold-and-green plaid couch that reminded him of a sofa his grandparents had when he was young. Just thinking about his grandmother still caused him heartache.

"Are you taking medication too?" Lee Ann grunted as she crossed one leg over the other.

"Uh, what? Medication? No, I don't—"

"I saw you looking at your watch." She raised a sculpted eyebrow.

Logan took a deep breath and forced himself to relax. He said a quick prayer, the same way he did with all his patients on the first day, asking God not to let anything happen to Lee Ann while under his care. "I guess I just feel like I need to be doing something." He smiled. "But I'm keen to chat."

She narrowed her eyebrows, frowning again. "Addison is my daughter. And I love her..." She paused, and Logan thought this sounded familiar. "But I don't need anyone to take care of me. I'm quite capable of getting around, taking my medication, and preparing my own meals. But when Addison first mentioned that I might need someone to stay with me, I thought that *she* might move in for a while, or at the least that she might come over every day to check on me. I was willing to play along with that scenario because…" She sighed, then waved a hand in the air. "Never mind. It doesn't matter. My point is, she's hired you so she doesn't have to come over every day. And the whole thing is really pointless. Does she think I might fall or a have a problem between ten in the morning and three in the afternoon, but not during the night?"

Lee Ann had a point, but Logan hoped she wasn't about to ask him to stay the nights too.

"Relax, Logan. I don't need you to stay the nights any more than I need you during the days." She chuckled. "And I can bathe myself as well." Logan felt himself blushing. "I just like to ruffle Addie's feathers sometimes. She's much too serious."

And beautiful. But Logan had to agree with Lee Ann. At first glance, Addison was eye-catching with her dark hair and eyes set against an ivory complexion with a tinge of natural color in her cheeks. But any hint of happiness was buried beneath a solemn expression. He noticed that she'd only smiled once and even that one had seemed sarcastic. Logan nodded.

"So, are you really a chef? Or did you just say that to impress my daughter?" Lee Ann was the exact opposite of her daughter. She smiled a lot.

Logan felt himself turning red again. "I'm not a certified chef, but I think I could compete with the professional blokes." He recalled the hours spent in his grandmother's kitchen.

"Where are you from? You have a lovely accent."

Logan got that a lot. He smiled. "Australia. New South Wales. But I've been here for seven years on work visas, so I like to think I sound a bit more like I belong here."

Lee Ann smiled. "Australia is on my bucket list." Her smile faded, and she got a faraway look in her eyes before she snapped her eyes back to Logan and slapped a hand to her knee. "So these meals you will be cooking…American or Australian?"

"Whatever you'd like. I can grill a mean American steak, and I can also whip up some balmain bugs, although I'm guessing I won't be able to find them here."

Lee Ann shriveled up her face. "No bugs."

Logan chuckled. "They're not actually bugs, more like lobster, and they're found in the shallow waters around Australia. Fresh fish was abundant where I lived, so I can cook fish a dozen different ways. But I have a very good recipe for split pea soup. It is my grandmother's and one of my favorites."

"I love pea soup, and I can't remember the last time I had it. Too much trouble to cook for just one person, and it's not something you usually find on a menu."

"I could make the soup, and then I can make you a lamington for dessert. It's a square chocolate sponge cake with a layer of icing and coconut. It's referred to as the national cake of Australia." He paused. "Do you have any allergies? I should have asked that."

Lee Ann clapped her hands together several times. "Fun, fun. I love trying new foods, and I don't know of anything I'm allergic to." She pointed to her right. "In the kitchen, there is a pad of paper on the counter by the phone. I keep an ongoing list of things I need at the grocery store. You just put whatever you need on the list, and I'll get it."

Logan tried to recall information on the agency list, and he was pretty sure Lee Ann wasn't supposed to be driving. "Do you…um…have a ride to the market?"

She glared at him for a few seconds. "Don't you dare tell Addie I'm driving."

Logan hung his head, shaking it, before he looked back up at her. "You had a stroke, and you took a nasty fall. I don't think you should drive."

Lee Ann continued to stare at him, but she didn't say anything.

"If you will allow me to take your list with me when I leave, I can pick up what you need and bring it back tomorrow. Perhaps we can plan a menu for the rest of the week. I'm happy to make enough so that you can have dinner as well as lunch." It had been a long time since Logan had cooked for anyone.

Lee Ann folded her arms across her chest, scowling like a child.

"Otherwise, I won't cook for you." Logan grinned a little. "Will this work for you?"

She kicked her foot into motion, still staring at him. "You don't get paid to do my grocery shopping."

"Hmm…" He rubbed his chin. "How can we make this right?"

"By letting me drive and not telling my daughter." There was a hint of a grin on her face, but Logan was pretty sure he could close the deal and keep her off the streets.

Chapter Three

Addison showed up at her mother's house close to noon. Not something she planned to make a habit of, but she felt compelled to check on the new guy. As usual, the front door was open. She knocked on the slat of the screen door twice before she let herself in. She was immediately hit with the most wonderful smell coming from the kitchen.

Logan was sitting at the table with her mother, both of them with their heads down fitting pieces of the puzzle. Glancing around, she was happy to see things tidied up, and on her way to the dining room table, she ran her hand across the hutch, pulling back nothing. Even the music box her father had given her mother decades ago was shiny. *Hmm…*

"Addie, if you've come to check on Logan, we're doing very well, thank you." Her mother lifted her head and smiled. "Or did you come to have lunch with us? We're having split pea soup."

"G'day, Addison." Logan looked directly at her, and she avoided his eyes for a few moments, then he drew her in like a magician with a wand. And it didn't help that his low, accented voice was also tender.

She forced herself to smile. "I can't stay for lunch, but it smells wonderful."

"Why can't you stay?" Mom looked up from the puzzle.

"I—I just can't. I work for a living, and I have appointments." She tossed long strands of hair over her shoulder, wishing she had a twisty to put her hair up. "Mom, I can't believe you're making Logan endure the heat in here, especially with the stove on. Maybe you can make an exception to your no-air-conditioning-until-July rule?"

Her mother was still rattling on about saving money on electricity when Logan stood up and walked to the window facing the beach. Addison followed him, and slowly her mother also joined them.

"I saw that man yesterday morning," her mother said as she leaned closer to the glass pane. "He was staring at my house, just like he is now. And, come to think of it, he was out there yesterday afternoon too."

"I'm sure he's harmless, Mom. Looks like he's even limping a little." Addison thought the fellow looked to be about seventy. "Maybe he's going to offer to paint your house. It needs it. I've told you I'll pay someone to do it."

"I don't need you to pay for it. I have money, but there are other things I'd like to do with it besides paint the house." Her mother kept her eyes on the man. So did Logan.

"Like what?" Addison finally asked. But Logan spoke up before her mother had a chance to answer.

"I'll go walk out there, casually, and see if I can find out what he's up to, since he's staring back at us." Logan eased around Addison and her mother. The screen door had barely slammed behind him when Addison's mom grabbed her arm.

"Is that man a gift from God or what? He looks like he stepped off of the cover of a magazine, and he can cook. And look how protective he is." She squeezed Addison's arm. "The fridge is full of ingredients to make authentic Australian food all week long."

"Mom, did you drive to the store?" Addison put a hand on her hip. "I told you that if you needed anything, I'll have someone do your shopping for you."

"Nope. Logan took care of everything. I gave him my credit card when he left yesterday, and today he showed up with everything on my list. He even bought the generic brands that I like. You always buy the name brands that are more expensive."

Addison never did anything right in her mother's eyes, so she just let the comment go. "It's not his job to shop for you, Mom."

"That's what I told him. So, we made an agreement. He does the shopping and in return, he gets two hours to help me with my puzzle."

Addison struggled not to laugh. "And he agreed to this deal? Sounds like a win-win for you. Not sure what he gets out of it."

"The boy seems to need permission to just relax. He's always nervous, moving around, and jittery.

Honestly, he makes me nervous with all that activity. But he seems calm and relaxed when we're working on the puzzle or when he's cooking."

"Normally, I would tell you that it's not safe to give a stranger your credit card, but since he came through an agency, I assume he's okay. But I hope you at least got a receipt from him."

"Yes, I did. And he'd only bought himself two pairs of trousers and three shirts."

Addison's eyes opened wide, but only until her mother grinned. "Ha, ha," she said, almost smiling herself. Then she held her breath and put a hand to her ear. "Could it be? I don't hear that kitchen faucet dripping."

"Did I forget to mention that Logan fixed that yesterday before he left?" Mom grunted as she stomped one foot against the wooden floor. "Addie, if you don't at least try to get a date with that man, then there is something *wrong* with you. Not everyone will trample your heart the way Connor did. It's been almost a year since the two of you broke up, and you haven't had one single date."

"Mom, Dad's been gone two years, and you haven't gone out with anyone either." It was the only comeback Addison could think of that might fend off her mother's matchmaking attempts, but her mother burst out laughing.

"I'm not twenty-seven years old. And let's face it. I had thirty-six years with your father, and as you well know, it wasn't all crumpets and tea."

That's an understatement. Addison had watched her mother run her father off emotionally long before he got cancer. Dad was probably ready to check out just to get away from her she thought, opting to keep quiet. She'd been biting her tongue a lot since her mother's stroke. In spite of everything, she couldn't bear it if anything happened to her too.

Mom put a finger against the window. "Look at that gorgeous man out there. And he seems as nice as he can be."

Addison stared as Logan talked with the man on the beach. "Guys that good-looking aren't always what they seem—I'm sure there's plenty wrong with him." She already knew of one flaw, he was the religious type. But she didn't dare get into that conversation with her mother. Addison had been raised in the church, and until her mother's stroke, Mom had attended church every Sunday. "Probably a lot of baggage too," she whispered.

Her mother wrapped an arm around her waist. "I'm going to pray that you open your heart to love again, Addie."

Addison fought to keep her eyes from welling up.

Logan had dropped his shoes on the porch. He leaned down and rolled his pants legs, sighing as the cool water lapped against his calves. When he straightened back up, he folded his arms across his chest and peered at the old man.

"You can't just stand here staring at the house like that." Logan glanced over his shoulder, glad to see that Addison and Lee Ann weren't still watching them from the window. "It makes people nervous."

"It makes *people* nervous, or it makes *you* nervous?" The old man stared toward the window again. "Yesterday was the first day I've felt well enough to walk the beach in months, to feel the warm sand between my toes, and…" He paused and smiled, still gazing toward the window. "…and to be able to see Lee Ann. Even if it's just from a distance. I don't think she's ever noticed me before. I've been walking up and down this beach and slowing down at her house for a long time, ever since I saw her sitting on the steps of her front porch." He paused again. "She waved, but that was over a year ago. I doubt she even remembers. I'm surprised that she noticed me twice yesterday and then again today." He smiled as he drew his eyes from the window back to Logan. "I'm gonna take that as a good sign. Maybe soon she'll come out here herself, instead of you." He grinned.

"I'm glad you're feeling better. I really am." Logan tucked his hair behind his ears, surprised the agency hadn't made him cut it. "But it's not safe for you and me to be hanging out together. You know that." He looked toward the window again, and in the distance, he could see Addison and her mother sitting at the dining room table. "Ronny said it's better if we stay apart, so that no one puts two and two together and figures out who we are."

"I really don't care if they do or not." The old man stormed off down the beach without looking back.

"You better care mate," Logan whispered as he watched the old man getting farther and farther away.

Chapter Four

Addison decided to pay her mother and Logan a surprise visit after showing a house nearby. As usual, she tapped twice on the door, then pushed the screen open. "Mom?"

Logan appeared from down the hall, smiling. "G'day."

"Your mum isn't here. I dropped her at the beauty salon. I'll pick her up at one."

"Is everything going okay?" Addison glanced around the house before looking back at Logan. She swallowed hard and reminded herself that beautiful outside doesn't mean beautiful inside. And yet she was allowing this man to care for her mother instead of doing it herself. "Is Mom behaving?"

"Yeah, all is well." Logan tucked his hair behind his ears. His long wavy blond hair that he wore incredibly well. "I'm not finding much to do around here at the moment, and we had an early lunch. I thought I'd go take a walk on the beach before I picked up your mum. Wanna go?" He nodded toward the window, toward a surf that was higher than normal for Galveston, but she was already shaking her head.

"No. I was just in the area and decided to drop by." She took a step backward as she pulled her purse up on her shoulder, then glanced at the water again, tempted by the beautiful day, recalling the feel of the sand between her toes. She couldn't remember the last time she'd walked along the beach, something she'd probably taken for granted her entire life, but never made the time for anymore.

"I know you want to go. It's gorgeous outside." Logan smiled as he moved toward the door, kicked his loafers off, and rolled up his slacks a few times.

Please don't take your shirt off. Addison looked out the window again, deciding maybe she could learn a little bit about the man she'd selfishly hired to look after her mother. She stepped out of her heels. "Why not?" She shrugged before she leaned down and rolled up her black slacks. When she straightened up, Logan was smiling.

"Ready?" He pulled the screen door open, and Addison slid by him, inhaling a spicy scent of aftershave. They were quiet until they hit the beach and he asked which way she wanted to go. She pointed to her left and decided not to waste any time.

"How'd you end up in Galveston?" She started walking at a slow pace, and he fell in step with her. Then it hit her. The last time she'd walked on the beach was with Connor. Old memories bubbled to the surface and she was glad that there were some good ones sprinkled in with the bad ones.

"Doesn't everyone want to be in the United States?" He smiled as he tucked his hair behind his ears again. Addison pulled a hair band from her wrist and twisted her hair into a ponytail. "Windier than usual, eh?"

Addison nodded. "But why Galveston? It's a great place with lots of history right on the ocean, but I'm just curious, why here?"

"I wanted to be near the water."

Addison slowed down and lifted up on her toes when the tide swept across her ankles, realizing she hadn't rolled her pants up enough and glad she didn't have any appointments the rest of the day. Her sleeveless blue blouse was sprinkled with ocean spray as well. They picked up the pace. "So, I saw on your application that you've worked for the agency for two years. What did you do before that? Mom said you've been in the States for seven years."

Normally, there wasn't anything Logan despised more than lying, although he'd done his fair share recently. But he chose his words carefully before he spoke, in an effort to be truthful. He would just have to omit a few things. "I came here on a work visa, as an analytic consultant. An accounting job, of sorts."

Addison grinned. "You don't look like the accounting type."

"Apparently, I wasn't." Logan kept his eyes forward as he spoke. "I changed jobs several times and eventually landed an engineering job. I don't get real stoked about math, but I'm pretty good with numbers, and I like to build things."

"How in the world did you go from engineering to home health care?" She smiled. "You don't look like the engineering type either."

He shrugged, sighed, and tried to buy himself some time, giving a partial version of the truth. "I like taking care of people. You have a beautiful smile." The moment he said it, he wished he hadn't, despite his desire to change the subject. He wasn't going to be here long enough to get involved with anyone. As soon as he had enough money, he'd pay Ronny to get him out of this mess. Even though he'd been questioning Ronny's tactics since he arrived in the United States. Logan would pray the Lord would forgive him for what he'd done.

"Um…thank you."

Logan glanced her way, unsure if the color in her cheeks was from the heat bearing down on them or if she was embarrassed. But he decided to take advantage of her hesitation and redirect the conversation. "Your mum said you sell houses, big houses. Did you go to college for that?"

She shook her head. "When I was in high school, I had a part-time job working for a real-estate company, and I just sort of never left. By the time most of my friends were graduating, I was making a nice living." She sighed. "And I knew my parents couldn't afford college anyway. At least, they couldn't ten years ago. My dad worked like a dog, but Mom never worked. She always said it was because Dad didn't want her to, but I'm not sure if that's true." Addison glanced his way. "I grew up in that small house. Dad got a great deal on it after a storm came through and the owners didn't want to do the repairs. That was before I was born. So, Mom doesn't have a mortgage or anything, and she's got a small savings account, but I try to help her as much as I can."

"I sense that she'd like to spend more time with you." Logan was stepping into an area he probably shouldn't go. "She talks about you a lot."

She scowled as she slowed down and turned to face him. "I'm surprised. But don't believe everything she says."

Logan clicked his tongue as he shook his head. "If you say so, but that's a shame. It's all been good. Except…"

She stopped and faced him. "Except what?"

"Your mum says you're uptight, never have any fun, and don't smile enough."

Addison slammed her hands to her hips. "That's not true. I'm *fun*. I'm not *uptight*. And you saw me smile earlier."

Logan shook his head again. "Nope. I don't see it. I don't think you have any fun." He should avoid flirting with her, but she made it so easy.

She plastered a huge, fake smile across her face. "See. I'm smiling."

When Logan started to laugh, she did too, and he pointed a finger at her. "See, now you're having fun." He paused, looked into her eyes. "With me." After a few moments, he forced himself to look away and started walking again. He'd dated a few girls since being here, but none seriously. He'd avoided getting close to anyone, especially the past couple of years.

He could see Addison out of the corner of his eye, watching him. There was something dangerous about this woman that made him want to know her better. And for him—that could be perilous.

Addison stepped over a jellyfish that had washed ashore, thankful she'd pulled her eyes from Logan just in time. She'd been stung three times in her life, a hazard of growing up on the beach. "That was close," she said, glancing over her shoulder. She wanted to know more about his background, how he'd gone from engineering to home health care. That seemed a big stretch. But then she saw the older man who had been staring at the house a few days ago shuffling toward them. She might not have recognized him if not for the blue baseball cap he was wearing, wisps of gray hair peeking out on either side. And he had a slight limp.

She nodded toward the man. "That's the guy who was staring at the house, the one you talked to, isn't it?"

Logan slowed his pace, then stopped. "Yeah. He's a harmless bloke. I think he just has a crush on your mum." He pulled a cell phone from his pocket, appeared to check the time, then put it back in his pocket. "Can you make it back okay? I think I'll run back toward the house so I'm not late picking up your mum. Maybe we can do this again." He winked at her and was gone.

Addison stood still as he disappeared down the beach. She didn't think it was close to one o'clock, but odd as his hasty departure was, she was pondering the wink and the earlier comment about her pretty smile. She waved at the man as he approached her and slowed down.

"Beautiful day for a walk on the beach," he said, tipping his cap as he walked by.

"Yes, it is." She took in his features. He had soft gray eyes, a pleasant smile, with teeth that might be too white to be the ones he was born with, and he had on a Dallas Cowboys T-shirt and a pair of white shorts. Addison's mother never missed a Cowboys game on television. *Hmm...* She spun around and jogged a few steps until she caught up with him. "May I walk with you?"

"Why, that would be lovely. Seldom does a pretty lady ask to walk with me down the beach." He smiled, and Addison smiled back at him, recalling what Logan had said.

"I saw you out in front of my mother's house the other day. You were talking to that man I was walking with. Do you know my mother, Lee Ann Burke?" Addison briefly wondered if maybe he was a stalker, but his kind eyes seemed to confirm what Logan had said, that he was harmless.

He chuckled. "I guess that young fellow musta thought I was trouble or something. But I've been walking the beach for a long time, and your mother and I have waved to each other, even though that was a while back. I took ill, though, and just recently resumed walking." He smiled. "She probably doesn't remember seeing me, but I couldn't forget that face if I tried. I asked around until I found out who that beautiful woman was. But your father had recently died, so I knew it wouldn't be good to come calling on her." He briefly tucked his chin as he adjusted the brim of his cap. "May he rest in peace."

Addison missed and loved her father, but a man in her mother's life might be the best thing—for Addison. Logan would eventually stop coming—a thought that interrupted her train of thought—and Addison wouldn't feel the need to check on her mother as much if she had a companion.

They kept walking but the man turned to Addison. "You're as pretty as your mother."

"Thank you," she said. "I'm Addison Burke." She extended her hand, and the man latched on with a firm handshake.

"William Sparks."

Addison paused. "I wonder...," she said. "Maybe you would like to meet my mother?"

He raised his eyebrows, a full smile filling his face. "I would like that very much."

As kind as this man appeared, she didn't know him, so she decided to make sure Logan was there when the introduction was made. Although, she didn't know Logan very well either.

"What about tomorrow at lunch? My mother fell recently, so we have someone coming to the house each day from ten to three; the caregiver is a chef of sorts—a huge bonus for us. I'm sure another person for lunch would be just fine. They eat around eleven."

"I think that would be lovely," he said, smiling even brighter.

Addison had never played matchmaker for her mother, and this might be a total bust. But at least she would be there to watch how it played out. And to see Logan again. The wink and compliment lingered despite the warning bells going off in her head. Not only was she unsure if she wanted to date anyone—even someone as handsome as Logan—but something wasn't quite right about him. Nothing she could put her finger on. Maybe tomorrow's lunch would help her put her finger on it.

Chapter Five

Logan thought he might lose his breakfast when the old man walked through the door at ten forty-five, and only seconds later, Addison pulled into the driveway.

"What are you doing here?" Logan whispered through clenched teeth, thankful Lee Ann was around the corner in the kitchen. Although, she emerged before Logan could get an answer from their guest.

"Hello, William. My daughter told me you'd be joining us for lunch." Lee Ann walked toward them at the same time Addison came through the front door. "Oh good. Everyone is here," Lee Ann said as she smiled and folded her hands in front of her. Normally, Lee Ann was in long walking shorts and a casual blouse or T-shirt. Today, she was wearing a knee length, black skirt with a tan and black blouse—and jewelry. Her dark hair was pulled into a bun, and her cheeks and lips were redder than usual.

After an awkward introduction, Logan took a deep breath and reminded himself to call the man William. Lee Ann had told him when he arrived at ten that they would be having Addison and one other person for lunch. He'd been hoping Addison wasn't bringing a date, but now he was wishing she *had* brought a significant other, instead of the man they know as William. It was easy to see that this was a romantic setup that needed to be foiled. But not only did Lee Ann dress for the occasion, the air conditioning was set at seventy-two when Logan arrived.

"Please, come and sit down at the dining room table. Logan is a wonderful cook, and today he has prepared a special dish that he learned to make from his grandmother." Lee Ann motioned to the table, already set for four. Logan had offered to bow out since Lee Ann and Addison were having a guest, but Lee Ann had told him not to be silly. *I can't believe the old man agreed to this.*

Logan walked back into the kitchen while the others sat down. He returned with a green curry chicken pie and a basket of Anzac biscuits for dessert. On his second trip, he returned with a pill bottle holding Lee Ann's morning pills that she'd forgotten to take before Logan arrived. Most days, the morning pills were still in the pillbox on the counter when he got there. Sometimes the nighttime pills were also still in there. Yesterday morning, he'd found the milk in the cabinet by the glasses instead of in the refrigerator. He'd brought a fresh gallon with him today. If Addison couldn't be with her mother, she'd been wise to hire someone.

Following a prayer, which Lee Ann always led before meals, he took time to study Addison while everyone began to fill their plates. She was in a blue pantsuit, and with her dark hair pulled into a bun like her mother's, it was impossible not to notice how much they looked alike.

"Logan, these biscuits are wonderful. I know you said they are for dessert, but I couldn't resist trying one now." Lee Ann passed the basket to the old man. "William, you must try these."

Logan resisted the urge to glare at *William* and instead focused on Lee Ann. "Thank you. They're an Australian staple, a sort of commemoration to the members of the Australian and New Zealand Army Corps who fought in World War I, thus the name Anzac."

William cleared his throat. "Wives used to send them to the soldiers because the biscuits would stay good for a long time since they don't have eggs in them." He smiled before taking another bite.

"Oh my," Lee Ann said. "How do you know this? Are you from Australia, too, because I certainly don't hear any accent?"

Logan held his breath as he waited for William to respond.

"No, no. But I spent a large part of my life in Australia. It's where I met my wife. It was a random encounter while vacationing there with friends." William made the sign of the cross. "God rest her soul. But I was born right here in Texas, not too far from here, Surfside Beach." He paused, frowning. "Although, there's never much surf, so I'm not sure how it got that name." Logan let out the breath he was holding and hoped that William would stop there. "Right now, I'm renting a small house down the beach from you." Glancing up at Lee Ann, Logan was sure William's eyes were twinkling, and after taking a quick look at Lee Ann, her interest seemed to match his. Logan was forcing himself to see the old man as William, repeating the name over and over in his mind so he didn't slip up.

After everyone gushed about the meal, Lee Ann excused herself to go smoke, and to Logan's surprise, William followed her. The old man despised smoking.

"Um…" Logan took a deep breath, choosing his words carefully. "If I didn't know better, I would say you are trying to set up your mum with that man."

Addison reached for another biscuit. "I guess you could say that." She took a dainty bite before she went on. "You said he seemed harmless and that he had a crush on my mother. And Mom needs to do something besides jigsaw puzzles all day. In fact, this is the first time I haven't seen a puzzle on the table for as long as I can remember."

Logan nodded, distracted as he was, and shoved in his last bite of chicken curry pie, glancing several times over his shoulder toward the porch where Lee Ann and her date were seated.

"Why? You don't think it's a good idea?" Addison peered across the table at him.

Logan knew it wasn't a good idea. "I—I just mean, you don't really know him. I said he *seems* harmless, but I don't know that for sure." *Lord, forgive me for the lie.* There wasn't a kinder man on the planet than their lunch guest, and

Logan knew this to be a fact. Guilt wrapped around Logan so tightly that on some days, he felt like he was suffocating. At those times, he reminded himself that his lies probably saved the old man's life, and he could only hope God would look kindly on that when Logan stood before Him one day.

"That's why you're here," Addison said around a small bite of biscuit she'd just taken. "In case he came at us with an axe or something." She chuckled.

Logan enjoyed the sound of her laughter, but he wondered if she'd still see him as a good guy if she knew the truth.

Addison pushed the chicken pie around on her plate, not a huge fan of curry. *In case he came at us with an axe or something* was meant to be a joke, but as all the color drained from Logan's face, Addison stopped chewing and stared at him. "I was kidding." She paused when he didn't look at her. "About the axe."

"What?" He gave his head a quick shake before he stood up. "Oh. Yeah. I know."

Addison eased out of her chair and began helping him clear the dishes. "How's Mom? Okay?" She followed him into the kitchen and waited while he put his dishes in the sink, then she added hers. "I saw that you had to remind her to take her morning meds."

Logan leaned against the kitchen counter and stuffed his hands in his pockets, avoiding her eyes. "Yeah, she forgets sometimes."

Addison stretched her neck to the left a little, trying to meet his eyes, but his head was down as he crossed his ankles. Finally, he looked up and sighed. "I know she's not supposed to drive, so I kinda feel like I'm ratting her out, but I think she went to church Sunday. Could someone have taken her?"

"I don't know. I guess she could have found someone. How do you know she went?" Addison went to the small kitchen table in the corner and pulled out a chair.

"There was a bulletin from Moody Methodist Church on the hutch with last Sunday's date."

Addison rubbed her left temple, grateful Logan had fixed the drip, but feeling a headache coming on anyway. "Yep, that's her church. I'll ask her about it when she comes in."

"Maybe wait until after Oliver leaves so you don't embarrass her." He paused, sighing. "Hopefully, someone drove her or she'll be mad at me for telling you. But I'd feel terrible if she got in an accident and I never said anything."

Addison nodded, then sat taller. "Who's Oliver?"

Logan pulled his hands from his pockets, turned around, and started rinsing the dishes. "What?"

"You said Oliver...not to embarrass her in front of Oliver."

He glanced over his shoulder. "Oh, what's that guy's name?" He snapped a finger. "William. Sorry, I forgot."

Addison looked out the window, but from the kitchen she couldn't see her mother and William. "I wonder how it's going out there. They seemed to hit it off during lunch."

"I don't know. They seem to be very different people."

"Opposites attract," she said as she stood up. In the recesses of her mind, where happiness once lived, she was hoping Logan would ask her to go for another walk on the beach. It was probably a terrible idea, but the thought lingered there anyway.

"I'm Catholic, not Methodist, but I don't mind taking your mum to church. I can drop her off and pick her up while I go to Mass, or I can just attend hers as a visitor for a while. God's at both places anyway." He turned around and winked at her. Again.

"It won't kill her to miss church while she's still recovering." Addison rolled her eyes.

Logan folded his arms across his chest and grinned. "Whoa…"

"What?" She put her hands on her hips. "I could take her. It's just…" Deciding she didn't owe Logan any explanations, she bit her bottom lip, but she could feel it trembling just the same.

"I'm sorry." Logan walked toward her and touched her arm, an action that sent her pulse racing. She took a step backward, still struggling not to cry. "Addison, seriously, I'm really sorry. I was getting ready to ask what you were so mad at God about, but first of all…it's none of my business, and second—I shouldn't have snickered like that." He paused, sighing. "It's just…you sound like I used to. I was angry with God for a long time. Years, in fact."

Addison didn't want to cry. She'd done enough of that. And she didn't even know Logan. "You know what? I want to walk on the beach." She recalled Logan's comments about her not having any fun and thought about why the comment had stung so much. In high school, she'd been voted Miss Congeniality because of her 'bubbly personality.' At twenty-seven, had life already taken its toll on her and hardened her into one of those people she swore she'd never become? "Actually, I want to run down the beach. I want to get wet, play in the water, and forget about everything else for a while." She slipped out of her sandals and slid them across the kitchen floor in his direction. "You in or not?" *I'll show you fun*. It was an angry thought, this newfound need to have fun, to frolic and waste time when she should be working or doing something productive. But the beach used to represent happy times—with her father building sand castles and even with Connor. And after searching her memories, she was able to recall plenty of times that she and her mother had walked the beach looking for shells when she was a kid.

Logan grinned, and Addison knew flirting with him was a mistake, but there was such emotion and tenderness when he spoke to her about God, as if in some small way he understood what she was feeling. She had no desire to continue that conversation, but she did have a desire to find out more about him. At the very least, she couldn't help but wonder if a thread of happiness was buried beneath her grief, longing to come to the surface.

"I wish I could, but this kitchen is a wreck, and if you'll recall...you are paying me to take care of your mum and keep things in order."

"That's right...via the agency, I am your employer, and I say we go walk on the beach." In a bold move and playful—*fun*—moment she grabbed his hand and pulled him through the living room, dropping his hand to open the screen door. Her mother and William both turned her way.

"Mom, since you have company, Logan and I were thinking we'd take a walk on the beach. Is that okay? I'll help Logan clean the kitchen when we get back."

Her mother's face lit up as she put a hand to her chest. "I think that would be lovely."

Of course you do.

Addison wrestled with her emotions—about her mother, Connor, her father, and everything in between—even God. And flirting with Logan and taking a little time to play might be a nice change. But first she wanted to ask Logan something. She'd almost mentioned it earlier to her mother, but she didn't want things to get awkward for her mother in front of William. Maybe Logan would know what happened to the antique music box that had always been on the hutch, the one Addison's father had given to her mother decades ago.

Chapter Six

Logan had decided a long time ago that he'd never understand women, and Addison Burke was driving the point home as she skipped ahead of him down the beach, twirling around, wading through the water, and smiling more than the woman had smiled since he'd met her. Her flowing white skirt hung past her knees, and a pink short-sleeved blouse was tied at her waist. In her bare feet, with her hands in the air, she reminded Logan of a ballerina, but perhaps a dancer who'd lost her footing somewhere along the way. Whatever the reason, seeing her letting go was enticing Logan to shed a little of the anxiety he'd built up over the past couple of years, so he jogged ahead to catch up with her. But when he got close to her, she took off running. He caught up to her with little effort, but pretended it was a struggle, grabbing her around the waist to slow her down.

They went down together in the sand, landing

face-to-face on their sides. They caught their breaths, and as he gazed into her eyes, he wondered what it was she was looking for. *The eyes are the mirror to the soul*, his grandmother used to say, a phrase Logan wasn't sure he understood until this moment. Inside the uptight and serious Addison, there was a playful child longing to be free. *Free of what, though?*

She propped herself up on her elbow and cradled her cheek with her hand, still facing him. As she stared at him for a few moments, he couldn't help but wonder what was about to come out of her mouth, and who would be doing the talking? Serious or playful Addison?

"If you could have one thing in the world...," she began, as she pushed her sunglasses up on her head and squinted. "What would it be? I mean, even if it was somewhere you wanted to go. If you had just one wish in the entire world, what would it be?"

Logan swallowed hard, even though he didn't have to think about it. "I'd ask God to grant me one more day with my grandmother."

She stared at him, then said, "Is that something God can do?"

Logan wasn't sure he wanted to talk about his grandmother with Addison. He cherished the memories and they had become sacred to him. But Addison's eyes pierced the short distance between them in the sand, and the whole "window to the soul" thing seemed more evident than ever.

"Sometimes, in my dreams, I see her cooking in the kitchen," he said softly, fond recollections dancing in his mind. "And every once in a while, she'll say, "Bub, you're gonna do great things some day. Stop worrying about me. I'm cooking with the Lord today." He paused, smiling, and tried to recall the last time he'd had the dream. "I guess that's as close as I've come to spending time with her."

"Sounds like you two were close." Addison brushed the wild strands of hair from her face. "I never knew my grandparents, on either side. My father's parents were killed in a car accident before I was even a year old, and my mother's parents weren't exactly the grandparenting type. They moved to Boston after my mom graduated from high school. I don't think she's talked to them in years." Barely smiling, she said, "When I was little, I would pretend I had regular grandparents. Silly, huh?"

Logan felt like she'd injected him with truth serum. Suddenly, he wanted to share everything, but he was wise enough to know he couldn't do that, no matter how much he wanted to. "No, I don't think it's silly. But my situation is the exact opposite. I was raised by my grandparents after my mother left me in their care, and I never knew my father. I'm not sure my mother did either."

"Did you ever see your mother?"

"Not very often. Holidays, sometimes birthdays. But when I got older, I saw less and less of her." Logan brushed loose sand from his cheek. "I never pretended like I had parents when I was little. My grandma more than made up for the fact that I didn't. She died almost ten years ago, and I still miss her."

"Will you go back to Australia?"

The fifty-million-dollar question. "One day I will." He paused. "Did you know Australia is on your mum's bucket list of places she'd like to travel?"

"No, I didn't. We're not very close. I mean, we try to be, but we just never get there."

Logan was quiet. He didn't want to pry, although he was tempted. Two older women in shorts and T-shirts went by them powerwalking, but otherwise they were alone except for some children in the distance building a sand castle. He moved to a sitting position, his knees bent, facing the water.

"I bet the beaches in Australia are beautiful, especially compared to Galveston." She pushed her lip into a pout. "I love Galveston, but we aren't known for having the prettiest beaches." She tossed her head toward the murky ocean, barely a tint of blue visible.

"It's gorgeous there." Logan fought the swelling of emotions that was almost enough to make him cry. "I'll go back someday. There's a place I went to on the first Friday of every month when I was a kid, and I kept up the tradition as an adult. And whenever I get back, I'll keep going there. It's a place called Jervis Bay. Over the years, it got a little touristy for my taste, but the White Sands Walk from Greenfield Beach to Hyams Beach is awesome, and for whatever reason, you usually don't see more than a handful of people on the trail, unless it's a holiday weekend. It takes about an hour to make the walk."

"It sounds wonderful, but why the first Friday of every month?"

Logan recalled the first time his grandmother explained First Friday devotions, but he wasn't sure how much detail to go into with Addison. "It's kind of a Catholic thing," he finally said. "…to recognize the Sacred Heart of Jesus."

She was quiet and seemed to be waiting, so he went on.

"The Sacred Heart depicts Christ's physical heart as a way to symbolize His divine love for humanity." He glanced at her and saw that he hadn't lost her yet. "My grandma and I did the White Sands Walk after Mass, our idea of offering extra reparations for our sins. But after her hip surgery, it was too hard to walk that far. But I kept going."

Addison nodded, then slowly rolled onto her back and pulled her sunglasses back over her eyes, presumably to return the child to wherever she'd so briefly come from.

Addison wished she could lie in the sand, listening to the sounds of the ocean forever. And she wouldn't mind if Logan lay there with her, telling her about beautiful places across the world that she hoped to see someday. But too many things were on her mind right now. And she wasn't ready to delve into a deeper conversation about God. Just the mention of God brought a wave of emotions that she didn't understand.

She slowly stood up and brushed sand from her skirt and blouse. "Did my mother say why Australia is on her bucket list?" As Logan rose to his feet, she wondered again about the missing music box on the hutch. "I wonder what else is on her bucket list."

"Ask her." Logan faced her. "What's up with the two of you anyway?" He raised a palm to her. "You don't have to tell me if you don't want to. It's just sometimes the tension when you're both in the same room is off the charts."

Addison blew out a long breath and slowly started back down the beach in the direction they'd come from. She should have known better than to try to have a little fun. Logan probably thought her frolicking earlier was childish anyway. The situation with her mother was complicated. A topic she'd rather avoid.

"I told you before, I love my mom. She's just difficult sometimes."

Logan was quiet. Maybe he didn't agree, but he didn't know her mother the way Addison did. Logan didn't see the way her mother had treated her father before he died.

"Hey…uh, there was a music box on the hutch in the living room. I didn't see it earlier. Did she move it? My dad gave it to her a long time ago." She hoped it didn't sound like she was insinuating that he took it. But her inclination to trust people was miniscule these days. Connor had seen to that.

"Uh oh." Logan stopped, and Addison lowered her sunglasses and looked at him over the rims. Slowly, he eased his own shades lower until they were eye to eye.

"Uh oh, *what*? Did it break? If you broke it, it's okay. Accidents happen."

They continued to look at each other for a moment before he pushed his glasses back up. Addison did the same.

"I had no idea it was a gift from your father. I made a comment the other day that it was a beautiful music box. She asked me if I thought it was worth anything, and I told her I had no idea." He took a deep breath. "She asked me if I'd take it down to the pawn shop on the Strand and see what I could get for it. So, I did."

Addison dug her toes in the sand and clenched her fist. "Why would she do that?"

"I don't know."

She let out a lungful of air, closed her eyes, and tried to steady her breathing. "How much did you get?"

She waited, and when he didn't answer, she asked again. "How much did you get for the music box my father lovingly gave to my mother, a gift she obviously felt no sentimental attachment to?"

Logan hung his head. "Forty dollars."

Addison began to tremble, despite the heat, and she wondered if Logan was telling the truth. "You have got to be kidding me."

"Nope." He looked up at her. "I'm really sorry. I just figured she was short on cash. I asked her why she didn't sell it on eBay or put it on Craigslist. I told her she'd probably get more, but she said she'd already tried."

Addison's jaw dropped. "She'd already tried *what*?"

"She said she'd already tried to sell it on both those sites."

Addison burst out laughing. "Uh, hardly. Mom barely knows how to email, so I doubt she'd know how to use either of those sites."

Logan hung his head again. "I'm starting to feel like a go-between for you and your mum. Addison, you need to talk to her and find out what's going on. But I can tell you this...she's been selling tons of stuff online just since I started. Several times I've taken things to the post office for her on the way home."

"Has she ever said why?" Addison unintentionally grunted after the question, which wasn't very ladylike, but she didn't care right now. "Is she that short on money?"

Logan took his glasses off, rubbed his eyes, then put them back on. "Again, I think you need to talk to her. We haven't discussed her financial status, and I certainly wouldn't inquire about such personal stuff. But..." Logan sighed.

"Oh no. What else? Just tell me." Addison took a deep breath and held it.

"Yesterday, she told me she listed her car for sale." He paused, but quickly added, "but maybe she thinks she won't be able to ever drive again."

Addison shook her head. "I never told her that. The doctor just suggested that she not drive for a month or two just as a precaution in case she were to have another stroke, which usually happens not long after the first one. But I would never have told her to sell her car."

Logan turned his head and stared down the beach and away from Addison. She tapped him on the arm. "Is she selling anything else I should know about?"

"You need to talk to her, Addison." Logan kept his gaze down the shoreline.

"I will." They started walking again, faster this time. After a while, she said, "So...she's selling tons of stuff. Like what else?"

Logan stared straight ahead. "Pretty much everything."

Chapter Seven

Addison waited for her mother to say goodbye to William, then she told Logan he could leave early for the day.

"Um, what about all the dishes in the kitchen? And—"

Addison waved him off. "It's fine. I'll take care of it. I need to spend some time with my mother."

Logan looked with sad eyes back and forth between Addison and her mother, as if he were being marched to the guillotine. Then he motioned for William to follow him out the door.

"That was rude, Addie." Her mother grimaced as she slipped out of a pair of tan sandals—which even sported a bit of a heel—that Addison didn't recall ever having seen. "I was enjoying William's company, and it's not your place to dictate visiting hours around here. This is *my* home. And good grief, what happened to you? You look like you've been rolling around in the sand." Mom grinned. "Were you and Logan rolling around in the sand?"

Addison looked down at her clothes, then chose a spot on the floor to sit down, leaning against the recliner. She stretched her legs out in front of her and crossed her ankles, waiting for her mother to get comfortable on the couch.

"Mother..." Addison rubbed her temples as she tried to steady her breathing.

"Well, I must be in trouble if you're calling me *Mother* instead of Mom."

"Did you pawn the music box dad gave you, the one on the hutch?" Addison nodded toward the piece of furniture that had been in that same spot her entire life, along with the framed seashell picture hanging above it.

"No. I asked Logan to pawn it." Her mother spoke softly, hesitantly, as she cringed a little. "Why?"

Addison drew in a deep breath before looking at her again. "Did that music box not have any sentimental value for you? Did you even take into consideration that Dad worked hard to buy you gifts?" She slapped a hand against the rug on the floor next to her. "And why are you selling everything?"

Her mother stiffened. "Addie, this might come as a surprise to you, but I don't have to run things by you. What I do with my things and my money is my business. And if this is about you paying for a babysitter for me, I never asked or wanted you to do that."

"Mom..."Addison lifted herself into the chair, knowing she'd leave a wet spot but not caring. "I know you don't have to tell me your business, but Logan said he thinks you are selling everything you own!" She flung her hands in the air, dropping them in her lap. "Why would you do that? Where are you going to live? Are you broke? You should have talked to me about this. I mean, even your car?"

Her mother tapped a finger to her chin, but was quiet for a few moments. "I'm going to travel."

Addison's eyes grew larger. "Like, uh...for the rest of your life? So much traveling that you need to sell all your possessions?"

Mom raised her chin. "I won't need these things where I'm going."

Addison slouched into the chair and put her finger to her temple again, thankful that the air conditioner was running, but knowing a migraine was coming. "Where are you going?"

"Anywhere I want."

Addison wished her father were alive right now. "So, to make sure I understand...you're going to sell everything, pocket the money, and travel the world? For how long? Until your money runs out? Then what? You'll expect me to support you?"

Despite harboring resentments toward her mother, Addison rarely showed any outward disrespect, and her mother's hurt shone across her face and her eyes watered. But it was still a question Addison wanted answered.

"Addie..." Mom blinked a few times. "I'm well aware that you make a tremendous amount of money for your age, a fact that I'm not always sure is in your best interest. But rest assured, I will never ask you to support me. I have money set aside for my travels.

The reason I am selling everything I own is so that I can move into an assisted living facility.

"A year ago, I would have thought I was much too young to consider something like this, but if I'm not too young to have a stroke, then I suppose I'm not too young to have someone nearby if I needed help. The facility is furnished, so I don't need all this stuff." She waved her arm around the room as if the things she'd collected her entire lifetime were nothing more than petty trinkets.

Addison tried to decipher what was happening. "So, you're selling the house too?"

Her mother sat even taller as she folded her hands in her lap. "Yes. And don't worry, you can have the listing."

Addison considered telling her mother that this house was small potatoes compared to what she was used to, but the sting of her mother's slap still lingered on her heart. "Do you think that's all I care about, the listing?"

Her mother's glare felt like a burn against Addison's skin. "No. I think you also worry that I'm being foolish with my money and that I'll become a financial burden to you, but I assure you my affairs are in order."

"Mom, calm down. I've never thought you'd be a financial burden, and even if you were, I would have helped you."

Her mother propped her elbows on her knees, folded her hands, and rested her chin on them as she leaned forward. "Addie, I don't need or want your financial help. All I've ever wanted is for us to be close and to have the type of mother-daughter relationship that seems to have eluded us over the years."

This was a conversation Addison had avoided for years, but maybe it was time to confront the elephant in the room. "Mom, I love you. But it was very hard for me to watch the way you treated Dad, especially when he was dying."

"Your father had a roof over his head and food to eat. He never missed a doctor's appointment, and I made sure that he took all of his medications. I gave him a sponge bath daily when it became necessary and shaved his face. And when he became too weak to wipe his own butt, I did that too. So, maybe you need to elaborate."

Addison swallowed back the lump in her throat, wishing she'd avoided having this inevitable conversation. "What about tenderness? What about love? You acted like you were his nurse or caregiver, but where was an ounce of compassion? And I don't mean just when he was sick! For as long as I can remember, Dad was nothing but loving and kind to you, and you gave him nothing resembling love in return!" *There. I said it.* Addison waited for relief to wash over her, but instead dread filled her every pore. Would this be the last straw, the one that pushed Addison and her mother so far apart that they'd never find their way back to each other? She waited for her mother to burst into tears, but instead, Lee Ann Burke stood up and pointed a finger an inch from Addison's face.

"Is this what the chip on your shoulder has been about? How I treated your father? The fact that I didn't toss his butt out on the street should be calculated into that bottle of bitterness you've been hauling around. But I'm tired of protecting him, for your sake or his. Your father was a lying cheat...and everyone around here knew it but you. I stayed humiliated for most of our marriage! And I know you think I was lazy and never wanted to work, but your father was insistent I be a good little housewife, and I think that was largely because he didn't want me frequenting any of the places he might be if I had a job in town. Places I might see him flaunting one of his many girlfriends. Oh, the affairs came and went. And the apologies were stacked on top of each other like the worthless words they were. Eventually, someone new always came along." Her mother fell onto the couch, and her face was so red that Addison feared she might have another stroke or worse. She sat quietly, wanting to find reasons for how this couldn't be true. Her mother could be a lot of things, but a liar wasn't one of them.

"Why didn't you leave him?" Addison still wasn't sure she believed these accusations, but as she pondered her mother's statements, flashbacks of her childhood came forth like a wrecking ball, one in particular. Elementary school—it was open house. Her mother excused herself to go to the restroom, and Addison's young teacher was showing her father Addison's latest artwork. She'd only been a kid, but something about her father's exchange with the teacher had left Addie feeling unsettled, though she didn't understand it at the time.

"I should have left him, Addie. I know that now." Her mother reached for a tissue on the end table and dabbed at her eyes. "But marriage is a sacrament, something I was totally committed to, and in my mind, it was best for you to grow up with two parents under the same roof."

"Why are you telling me this now?" Addison fought the tremble in her bottom lip.

Her mother offered the slightest hint of a smile, then whispered, "Because you asked."

Logan paced the small living room in the old man's house. He'd reprimanded him all the way home.

"Quit pacing, Logan. Just sit down and relax."

Logan shook his head. "You're unbelievable. I shouldn't even be here, at your house. You know what Ronny said, that our chances of getting caught are highest when we're together. And you're going to blow it for both of us by playing kissy-face with the woman I work for."

"Well, there's been no kissing, but I'm hopeful." The old man grinned.

"This isn't funny. If you don't want to spend the rest of your life in jail, you'd better take this seriously."

The old man pounded a fist against the coffee table. "I'm tired of all this. I'd rather go to the authorities and do my time in jail if I have to. I can't keep up this charade. I finally have a chance with Lee Ann, and you're trying to make me give up the one thing that gives me hope. Can't an old man hold on to a shred of happiness?"

Logan sat on the couch next to him, compassion and fear all wound up in a tight ball in his stomach. "Maybe it's the price we paid to keep you alive."

The old man turned to him, tears in his eyes. "This isn't living. This is existing."

Logan leaned back against the couch, and both of them stared straight ahead. He knew the old man's comments were true. Much of the time, Logan felt like he wasn't living either. He was always looking over his shoulder. "If we see this through until Ronny can get things worked out, then—"

"Ronny, Ronny, Ronny. I'm sick of hearing what Ronny's gonna do!" The old man's arms flailed above his head. "We're in this mess because of Ronny. We should have just faced the music two years ago. It wouldn't have been near as bad as facing prison. I'd rather go to prison for the rest of my life than feel like I'm always on the run."

"What about me? Do you want me to spend the rest of my life in prison too?"

The old man turned toward him. "It's not like we murdered anyone, ya know? Maybe we do our time for what we've done, then get on with our lives the way the Lord intended us to, without a bucketful of lies strapped to our backs." The man sighed. "Don't get me wrong. I'll forever be grateful to you for what you did for me. You saved my life. But this just isn't living."

Logan stared at the elderly man's watery eyes, feeling his own eyes tear up, then said, "I just need a little more time and money, then I promise I'll get us out of this mess. Please, Grandpa. Just trust me."

Chapter Eight

Addison pushed all the pictures from her bed with one sweep of her arm, sending them flying in every direction in her bedroom. Then she walked around and stomped on each one. The photos with Connor's face staring up at her, she ground those beneath her heel. It was one of those things that a girl would never want to go public with, but a ritual that gave her a level of satisfaction just the same.

When she was done, she flung herself onto the bed and cried. But this time, she wasn't just wallowing in her own self-pity, but crying for her mother as well. She glanced at her phone on the table by her bed; she hadn't talked to her mom in four days. Addison was curious if her mother had fired Logan since he'd spilled Mom's secrets. But she hadn't been curious enough to call and find out. She'd missed two calls from her mother, but she was still sorting things out in her mind.

She wasn't sure what upset her more, that her father had done this to her and her mother for years, or that her mother hadn't told her. She decided that she was more upset with her father. *Men cheat.*

Fifteen minutes later, she was dressed and out the door. By the time she arrived at her mother's house, she still didn't know what she was going to say. She pulled the screen open and tapped on the wooden door, a sure indictor that the air conditioning was running.

Her mother answered the door wearing a modest white sundress and flat white sandals. "Well, this is a surprise." She stepped back so Addison could enter, then closed the door behind her. "I wasn't going to drive if that's what you're worried about."

"Then how were you going to get to church? I wasn't even sure you still had a car." Addison fought to keep the tremble from her voice. "You look very pretty." She blinked her eyes a few times to push back the tears pooling in the corners.

Her mother put a gentle hand on each of Addison's arms. "Addie, sweetheart...I just never told you because you idolized your father. I didn't want to take that from you."

Addison didn't try to stop the tear that slid down her cheek. "You should have told me. All this time, I've been awful, blaming you for everything that went wrong between you and Dad."

Mom smiled. "And it was a burden I was willing to carry if it kept you from any further upset. But maybe I was wrong."

Addison opened her mouth to speak, but nothing would come out. She wanted to tell her mother she was sorry, but a knock on the door took her away from her thoughts. "Who's here?"

"Logan. He offered to take me to church. He's a little late. We were supposed to run a couple of errands on the way to church." She shook her head, but grinned. "If that boy has one fault, it's that he's always running behind." Mom's grin spread into a full smile. "But it's a fault I'm willing to overlook, and today...it worked out for the best." She pulled the door open. "Hi, sweetie. Come on in."

Addison frowned. *Sweetie?* But then her eyes fixated on Logan with his gorgeous blond hair neatly groomed, and he was wearing black slacks, a dark blue shirt, and a tie. Addison glanced down at her blue jeans, heeled sandals, and short-sleeved red blouse, feeling underdressed, but relieved she wouldn't have to take her mother to church.

"Addie came to take me to church." Mom folded her hands in front of her, and it was impossible not to hear the joy in her voice.

"No, no. I didn't want her to drive herself." She rolled her eyes, but smiled. "But since you're here, I'll let you two go." She eased around Logan, but he caught her by the arm.

"Why don't we all go?" Logan dropped his hand, but raised an eyebrow.

Addison shook her head. "No, that's okay. Church isn't really my thing." She glanced at her mother, who hung her head, then Addison looked back at Logan. "But you two go."

"Addie, it's Logan's day off, and I'm sure he'd rather go to his own church." Her mother sighed. "Wouldn't you, Logan?"

Logan opened the door, pushed the screen open, and in a firm voice said, "I'm taking the two prettiest ladies in town to church, then out to eat at Shrimp 'N Stuff."

Mom clapped her hands. "How wonderful. I haven't eaten there in a long time, and it's one of my favorite places on the island."

Addison hadn't been to Shrimp 'N Stuff in years either. It was a super casual, cheap place for seafood, and not somewhere she frequented. But they served some of the best seafood in Galveston. Her mouth watered just thinking about it. *How bad could one hour of church be?*

Logan followed Lee Ann down the aisle of the church, Addison lagging far behind. He figured she'd make a run for it any minute. Her face was white earlier when they approached the door. He glanced over his shoulder to make sure she was still coming, and she was. Shuffling slowly down the aisle.

"How long's it been since she's been to church?" Logan asked Lee Ann as they eased their way into a pew.

"A long time," Lee Ann said as Addison caught up to them.

After a few minutes of silence, Logan whispered to Addison. "Don't look so scared. I promise you'll come out of this in one piece."

She glanced at him, and barely offered up a weak smile. "I'm only here for the fish later."

Prior to the service starting, Logan prayed about the choices he'd made recently and once again, he asked God to forgive him for the lies, and to guide him back to a place where he could live an honest life. Then he prayed for continued good health for his grandfather.

He glanced at Addison. She didn't appear to be breathing. Logan could clearly recall a time—not that long ago—when he fell away from God. When the Lord wouldn't heal his grandfather. His grandmother had passed, and the thought of losing the other most important person in his life had been overwhelming, especially because Logan had prayed and prayed for God to heal the old man. But instead of healing his grandfather, God had shown Logan another path. And his grandfather had gotten better. But now it took every ounce of faith Logan had to trust God to guide his journey. Logan feared there must have been a fork in the road somewhere, because it sure felt like he'd taken a wrong turn.

He cleared his thoughts so he could focus on the service, and even though it was quite different from the Catholic Mass he was used to, he could feel the Holy Spirit moving him, and when he heard Addison sniffle, he cut his eyes in her direction without moving his head. Her eyes were filled with tears, and Logan had no way to know if they were happy or sad tears. Church had a way of doing that to a person, especially if you hadn't been in a while. Without giving it much thought, he found her hand and grasped it in his. She squeezed back, but kept her eyes straight ahead. It was an odd moment. Logan didn't know her very well, but as he held her hand, he felt like he could feel her pain, and he had an overwhelming desire to fix whatever ailed her.

Logan's grandmother had told him since he was a young boy, that he was a fixer. At times it had been more of a curse than a blessing—the ends he would go to in an effort to "fix" a person or situation.

Addison abruptly let go of his hand, eased out of the pew, and hurried down the aisle. Logan looked at Lee Ann as a pained expression fell across her face, and he stepped out of the pew to go after Addison.

Mistake, mistake, mistake. Addison rushed out the door and into the Texas heat, breathing in the smell of the ocean, and hoping her mother or Logan didn't come looking for her. But when she heard the large, wooden church door close behind her, she turned to see Logan standing on the steps.

"I'm fine. I just needed some air." She waved a hand toward him. "I'll be back in a minute." Dabbing at her eyes with her finger, she turned away from him, but she could hear footsteps getting closer, until he was close enough to inhale the spicy scent of his cologne. He gently put his hands on her shoulders.

"What's wrong?" he asked in a whisper, the feel of his breath sending a shiver down her spine.

"I don't know." It was the only answer she had. "I feel so stupid." She turned to face him, and the tenderness that shone in his expression melted her resolve, and when he pulled her into a hug, she laid her head against his chest. "Who cries in church?" Right now, she just wanted to stay in the comfort of his arms, a man she barely knew.

Logan eased her away, moved strands of loose hair from her face, then dabbed at a tear on her cheek.

"I think that sometimes, when we've been away from God for a while, we're overwhelmed by the way He welcomes us back with pure love and forgiveness. The Lord's heart is always open and welcoming to us, even if we've turned our backs on Him."

She hung her head, then looked up at him. "I went through a bad breakup, and my dad died, all at the same time. It was just too much, and I prayed and prayed and prayed for peace, for comfort…and nothing. I just kept sinking into a bottomless pit of despair. So, I threw myself into my work, and I stopped talking to God. How can I get past that?" She paused, sighed. "And do I even want to? God let me down at a time when I needed Him most. What if He does it again?"

Logan cupped her cheeks in his hands, a slight smile playing on his beautiful face. "God doesn't let us down. He gives us choices, free will. It's up to us whether or not we choose the path He's chosen for us. And much of the time, we veer off on our own journey, which never leads us to true happiness. But it's the struggles that bring us back to God and closer to Him than we were before."

"So, we need to go do a bunch of bad stuff or make poor choices, then God will reel us in and make it all better?" She paused, holding up one finger, even though Logan was still close enough to kiss her, a distracting but lovely thought. "Why do we even have to go through the bad? Why can't He just lead us to the good? Connor cheated on me, and I was devastated that my dad died." She sighed. "I'll always love my father, but apparently he didn't do my mother right either, and now I'm eaten up with regret about the way I've treated my mom the past few years." She paused. "And I'm furious with my father."

"Anger and regret will feed on you like a hungry predator, leaving you raw and unable to forgive yourself. Believe me, I know."

Something about Logan's voice made her sense he was facing his own demons. "I can't just stand here and make a conscious decision that I'm going to start praying again, that I want God back in my life."

Logan's face broke out into a big smile. "Sure you can. It's that easy."

She stared into his eyes, longing for his lips to just gently brush against hers, which seemed wrong in light of the subject matter and the fact that they were ten feet from the church. She eased herself away, putting an arm's length between them.

"Do you trust God?" she asked in a shaky voice.

"I do." He looked away from her, his gaze set to his left. "I disappoint Him over and over again. I make bad choices, step off the right path, and all the while God is there to lead me back to Him." His eyes brimmed with tenderness when he looked back at her. "And right now, that's exactly what I'm doing. I'm waiting. I'm waiting for answers. I'm waiting for him to tell me what to do, to tell me how I can get home."

Addison held her breath as Logan's eyes watered up. More was going on with Logan than he was admitting. "Home to Australia?" she finally asked.

"Home to *Him*." He paused. "And yes. Home to Australia."

She swallowed hard, and as he stepped closer to her, warning bells sounded all over the place. *He wants to go home. Don't get close to him.* "Just get on a plane and go home," she whispered as he grew even closer.

"I wish it was that simple."

She waited for him to kiss her, knowing she'd let him, but he took a step back and held out his hand to her. "Maybe we should both go back in. And instead of praying for ourselves, why don't we pray for each other?"

Addison liked that idea. Something about Logan screamed out to her that he needed prayers, and praying for someone else was within her comfort zone today. "Okay," she said softly.

She took his hand and together they walked back into the church, and when he squeezed her hand, she squeezed back again.

What's happening?
With me and God?
And...with me and Logan?

Chapter Nine

Logan was in dangerous territory. Not only had church and Shrimp 'N Stuff become a regular Sunday outing for Logan, Lee Ann, and Addison—but Logan's grandpa had started attended the Methodist church with them too. One big happy family.

It was bad enough that Logan and his grandfather were spending time together, something Ronny had said to avoid, but Logan was starting to have some fairly serious feelings for Addison. He'd stopped himself from kissing her several times. He loved watching her spiritual journey and the healing relationship developing between Addison and her mother. But everything else had disaster written all over it.

He knocked on his grandfather's door after work one day.

"Good, I'm glad you're here." Grandpa shuffled toward him in a pair of gray sweatpants and his

Cowboys T-shirt. "What do you think?" He winked. "It's not real. You think she'll be able to tell?"

Logan's heart rate tripled. "Surely that isn't what I think it is."

"Of course it is. I'm going to make an honest woman out of Lee Ann."

Logan glared at his grandfather, glanced at the ring, then back at the crazy old man. "She doesn't even know your real name. How can you possibly think about proposing? Not to mention you've only been hanging out with her for a few weeks!"

"The heart knows what the heart wants, and my heart wants Lee Ann Burke. So quit yelling." The old man slammed the ring box shut and huffed as he walked off.

Logan fell into his grandfather's recliner, covered his eyes with one hand, and slouched into the worn leather. "I gave Ronny the money to buy back our lives, so to speak. We're going home."

"I'm not going anywhere without Lee Ann."

Under different circumstances, Logan would have been thrilled that his grandfather had found love again. "Do you really think she will marry you when she finds out the truth?"

"I know she will. It's that kind of love." His grandfather sat down beside him. "I'm a blessed man, Logan. I told Lee Ann I love her, and she told me she loves me too. The Lord is giving me another shot at happiness."

"Grandpa...listen to me. You're going to be marrying her in a jail cell if we don't handle this the right way. Can you please just sit tight until I figure out what to do?"

"I don't like that Ronny fellow. I don't think he's steered us right from the beginning." Grandpa pointed a crooked finger at Logan. "Something's not right."

"There are a lot of things that aren't right. Where do you want me to start?"

Addison stared at the place where the television used to be. "I can't believe you sold your TV too." She glanced around the empty house as she slung her purse on the couch; the only piece of furniture left. Most everything was gone or packed in boxes. She'd been to breakfast with her mother and didn't have any appointments today, so she'd been lingering around until Logan showed up. This morning her mother had tripped walking into the café, and later confessed she'd forgotten to take her nighttime meds again.

"They have a television at the assisted living facility, but..." Mom grinned, and Addison felt like she and her mother had reached an entirely new level in their relationship, more like girlfriends. Addison had a couple of girls she hung out with from time to time, but most of them were married and had husbands and children. "...but I think William is going to propose."

Addison stopped breathing for a few moments. "What? Are you kidding?"

Her mother reached for both of Addison's hands and squeezed. "I love him, Addison. I really do. Would you approve?"

Addison's eyes filled with tears. "I can't think of anyone who deserves to be loved and happy more than you." She fell into her mother's arms and thanked God that her mother was finding some joy in her life. Praying had become a part of her routine. She didn't know if God was answering her prayers, but she was practicing patience, like Logan said. *Logan. A force to be reckoned with.* Some days she thought he might be madly in love with her, and other times he seemed to avoid her like the plague.

"Maybe I'm wrong, Addie, but he's hinted about marriage a couple of times."

"I'm happy for you, Mom, but you haven't been seeing him for very long."

"The heart wants what the heart wants, as William would say. And Addie…" Her mother shook her head. "We're not getting any younger, and William has almost ten years on me."

"I hear you."

Mom cleared her throat. "So. What about you and Logan? William and I can see the spark between you two."

Addison shook her head. "No. It's not like that with us." *I wish it were.*

"For someone whose nature seems so laid back, that boy has a nervousness about him that makes it hard for him to relax."

Addison knew exactly what her mother was referring to. She'd start to feel that things were moving in a more romantic direction with Logan, then he'd look over his shoulder, or seem to remember something he'd forgotten, and he'd back off. "Maybe he doesn't like me…enough." *And can I trust him not to break my heart?*

"Hosh posh! That's silly. I catch the guy staring at you all the time."

Addison smiled. She'd caught Logan gazing at her more than once, and it always sent a warm wave over her. "Well, he sure doesn't act on it."

"Logan hasn't dated anyone seriously in over two years. He shared that with me recently when I tried to discreetly pry into his personal life." Mom cupped her chin with her hand. "I didn't get a sense that he was recovering from a broken heart or anything. But I know he's trying to save money, so that might be part of his hesitancy." She paused as her expression fell flat. "Uh oh. I know what it is."

Addison straightened on the couch. "What? And how do you know so much about Logan anyway?"

"You are paying that agency good money for him to spend a lot of time with me. We have lots of time to talk."

Addison had considered cancelling the agency service, but she was terrified she might not see Logan again. "You said you know what it is that's holding Logan back. What is it?"

"You already know what it is. He wants to get home to Australia. That's a long way to carry on a long-distance relationship. I think he is protecting his heart. And protecting yours too."

Addison shrugged. She'd considered that possibility. And despite her growing feelings for Logan, she'd felt herself holding back for those same reasons.

"But just remember…the heart wants what the heart wants." Her mother pulled her into another hug.

Addison swallowed back a knot in her throat. Again. How could she have not seen the beautiful and deserving woman her mother was? Addison's anger with her father wasn't going to go away over night, and Logan had said that if she forgave her father, it would give her peace. She was trying.

"I hear a car pulling in. Must be Logan." Addison pulled a compact out of her purse and checked her lipstick.

"So, that's why you've been loitering. You were just waiting for Logan." Her mother giggled, but didn't move from her spot next to Addison on the couch. "He lets himself in."

Addison tossed the compact back in her purse, but glanced at her mother when Logan knocked. "He's probably not walking in because he sees my car out there."

They both lifted themselves from the couch and moved toward the door.

"I'm so glad you've been running the air conditioner," Addison said, shaking her head. "That's why no one ever visited you before."

"Really? Because I think there were other reasons you didn't spend much time here as well." She slapped Addison on the butt as if she were a small child.

"Hey," she said, jumping as her mother opened the door.

A heavyset, middle-aged woman with salt-and-pepper hair was standing on the other side of the screen.

Addison's mother spoke first. "Can I help you?"

"I'm Evelyn. The agency sent me."

"No, no, no," her mother said, wagging a finger at the woman. "Logan has been coming since the beginning, and I really don't want to train someone new."

"Mrs. Burke, I've got many years of experience, so please don't worry." The woman pointed to a file folder she was holding. "Would you like to see my references?"

"Um…no, dear. Just go back to the agency and tell them to send Logan." Mom nodded and was about to close the door when the woman cleared her throat.

"Mrs. Burke, the man who was coming here doesn't work there anymore."

Her mother brought a hand to her chest. "Of course he does. There's some confusion somewhere."

Evelyn shook her head. "No, ma'am. I'm sure. They specifically said I am replacing someone who got fired."

Her mother lightly stomped her foot. "This is ridiculous, but I'll get it straightened out. I don't need anyone here today anyway. My daughter is here." She nodded to Addison. "Bye, now."

After Addison's mother slammed the door in the woman's face, she walked to the phone. "I'll call the agency." She dialed the number while Addison wondered how Logan could have gotten fired. *Maybe for always being late?*

"A recording picked up," her mother said as she put the cordless phone back in the charger. "I don't have time to wait for the next available associate." Mom paced back and forth a few steps. "I can't imagine why Logan would have been fired." She picked up the phone again and dialed. "I think we should just go to the agency, but I need to call

William first. He mentioned coming over here, so I need to let him know we're leaving."

A moment later, her mother set the phone in the holder, the color having drained from her face.

"Mom, what is it?" Addison moved toward her.

"I—I don't know. That's odd." Her mother blinked her eyes a few times. "A recording said William's phone number has been disconnected. What do you think that means?"

Addison took a deep breath. "I don't know. Maybe he didn't pay the bill. But right now, I think we should head to the agency. Maybe leave William a note on the door, in case he shows up."

They both picked up their purses from the couch and headed out.

Addison had a sick feeling in the pit of her stomach.

Chapter Ten

Addison held tightly to her mother's hand as they sat facing the administrator of the home health care agency, a woman her mom had gone to school with. Addison was too stunned to offer much comfort to her mother.

"Let me get this straight." Addison finally said. "Both Logan and William outstayed their visas and were deported? And William is Logan's grandfather?"

The woman on the other side of the desk—Nancy—nodded. "Apparently, they came here so that William could participate in a cancer trial being offered. William thought he had dual citizenship. He was born in Texas, but married in Australia. Logan came here on a five-year work visa. But just as they were preparing to head back to Australia, William had a relapse, so they didn't leave when they were supposed to. So, Logan had outstayed his visa, and there was a problem with William's paperwork with regard to dual citizenship." Nancy hung her head, sighing, before she looked at Addison's mother. "Lee Ann, I could get in big trouble by telling you all this. And I'm not even sure I'm explaining it all correctly. There was another man involved that seemed to have lead them astray and encouraged them to sign some things they shouldn't have. He was their sponsor to come here."

Addison's mom waved Nancy off, and Addison didn't know which question to start with, but at least they weren't deported because they'd committed some horrible crime. She squeezed her mother's hand. "See, Mom, it isn't so bad."

Her mother let go of Addison's hand and dabbed at her face with a tissue Nancy had given her. "If William has dual citizenship, why did he have to leave?"

Nancy leaned back in her chair, slipped off a pair of reading glasses, and sighed again. "I don't know all the details about William's status, just that there was a problem with his paperwork. But I'm afraid there's more, Lee Ann."

Addison's heart flipped in her chest. "What else?"

Nancy spoke with a kind, sympathetic voice. "We all really liked Logan, so this is sad news for us as well. Logan and William had paid someone to establish fake identities, so that William could be treated for his cancer when he relapsed, instead of taking a chance that they might be deported. They'd started out in Houston, but that's how they ended up in Galveston, at UTMB, for treatment. There was another cancer trial specifically for the type of cancer William had at UTMB. They were both facing jail time, but from what I've been told, the judge was lenient in light of the circumstances. He told them they could both go home to Australia, but they'd never be permitted back in the United States."

Addison's mother sobbed quietly to herself as Addison fought her own tears. Then it hit her. "Fake identities? Who are they, then? If they aren't Logan and William?"

Nancy leaned forward in her chair. "I don't know who they are. I had to pry the information out of the person who brought us the news. But the woman wouldn't tell me their real names."

"No, no, no." Her mother spoke loudly. "Are you telling me that you don't know what William's real name is? How will I get in touch with him? Is William cancer-free?"

"I'm sorry, Lee Ann. That's all I know. And I had to really push hard to find out that much." Nancy stood up, an indicator that their time together was ending. The woman had bags underneath her eyes, and Addison suspected this had been quite an ordeal for the agency as well. Her mother darted out of the room, and Addison lifted herself from the chair, reached across the desk, and shook Nancy's hand.

"I need to go take care of my mother. Thank you for telling us this much."

"Good luck. I can tell Lee Ann is heartbroken."

Addison sighed, nodded, and left Nancy's office, knowing she needed to be strong for her mother, even though her own heart was broken. She found her mother standing outside near an ashtray, just staring down at it. It was then that Addison realized that she hadn't seen her mother smoking lately.

"You know, I quit smoking for that man." Mom sniffled, raising her eyes to Addison's. "I felt like I had something to live for."

Addison blinked her eyes a few times. "I'm so sorry, Mom. So, so sorry."

"I don't even know his name!" She stomped a foot, then raised her eyes to heaven. "Why is God doing this to me? Don't I deserve some happiness?"

Addison wanted to tell her mother that God works in ways they don't understand. If she'd learned anything at all from Logan and her times in church, it was that each person had their own individual relationship with God, and as with all relationships, sometimes there was conflict. Her mother would have to work through this in her own way. Addison recognized having the thought, but also knew that she was struggling with what had happened as well, questioning how God could give her and her mother a glimpse of happiness, only to snatch it away. Then she remembered something.

"Mom. I think William's name might be Oliver."

Her mother's eyes grew round. "Oliver? He doesn't look like an Oliver. He looks like a William."

Addison shrugged. "Maybe, but I heard Logan— or whatever his name is—accidentally refer to him as Oliver."

Mom grabbed Addison's arm. "Do you know his last name?"

"No. I'm sorry. You're going to just have to wait to hear from him."

"What if I don't?"

Addison could kick William—Oliver—for hurting her mother like this. "Then it wasn't meant to be," she said softly. Her mother started walking to the car, and Addison slowly followed.

Jack climbed out of bed in possibly the most bittersweet moment in his life. He'd never been happier to be home in Australia, but his heart hurt, wondering what Addison and Lee Ann must be thinking. Such a betrayal, even if it had all been in an effort to save his grandfather's life.

"Jackson, I made dippy eggs with vegemite soldiers for breakfast," Grandpa hollered from the kitchen.

It should have been music to his ears, to know that an Australian breakfast was being prepared by his grandfather in their own kitchen, but Jack wasn't sure he could stomach much of anything.

"You're a chipper mate this morning," he said to his grandfather when he walked into the kitchen.

"Can't cry over spilled milk," the old man said. "Just gotta clean up the mess an refill the cup." He placed a plate in front of Jack. "Besides, I have a letter all ready to put in the mail to Lee Ann."

"Why don't you just call her?" Jack pulled the soldier toast from the dippy eggs and took a bite.

His grandfather sat down with his own plate. "If she's going to reject me, I'd rather read it in a letter. Besides, writing a letter is a chance to really tell her how I feel."

"You do understand that you can't ever go back to the United States, right?" Jack took a sip of coffee the old man had brought him.

"I know." He blew out a breath of frustration. "All that dual citizenship stuff took place fifty years ago. I have no idea if I did it wrong or what happened, and that Ronny fellow didn't help our cause. But there's nothing keeping Lee Ann from coming here."

Jack grunted. "Nothing but a mound of lies and betrayals."

"Jackson…" Only Jack's grandparents had ever called him that, and despite the situation, he welcomed hearing it again now that they were home. It was familiar. "I am alive and cancer-free. I'm not in jail. And I am in my own kitchen. So, I praise God for these things. My life is never going to be complete without Lee Ann, though." He paused, scratched his chin. "Are you going to contact Addison?"

Jack should his head.

"Why? I know you care for that girl."

Jack had spent the past three days in and out of a time warp of jet lag, his thoughts jumbled, his heart hurting. But in the end, he'd made a decision. "Addison had a bad breakup with her last boyfriend. The guy cheated on her. And she just recently found out some things about her father. More betrayals. And now me. You're right. I do care about her." *I think I'm in love with her.* "But we weren't around each other long enough for me to make a lasting impression on her, Grandpa. I feel like it's kinder to let her go."

His grandpa finished chewing a piece of toast. "But did she make a lasting impression on *you*?"

"It doesn't matter. Addison is more rigid than her mother, and I don't see forgiveness coming easily to her about this." He set the toast down. "I feel like I need some time out of my head."

"Last time you said that, you headed to Spain and walked five hundred miles."

Jack recalled his pilgrimage, the Camino de Santiago. It had been one of the most rewarding spiritual journeys of his life. When he closed his eyes, he could still recall laying eyes on what was believed to be the shrine of the apostle St. James the Great in the Cathedral of Santiago de Compostela. He was lost in memories when his grandfather spoke up again.

"Well, at least we have money again."

Jack forced himself to scoop up another bite of dippy eggs with his toast, even though he wasn't sure it was going to stay down. "I know. I messed up."

Grandpa chuckled. "Yeah, we weren't very good criminals. We should have thought to transfer funds before we decided to change our names."

They ate in silence for a while, then his grandpa burst out laughing again. "If I marry Lee Ann, Addison will be your stepsister. If things had worked out with you and Addison, would she have been your wife and stepsister? Would she have been my stepdaughter or daughter-in-law?" Still smiling, he tapped a finger to his chin. "Will you be Lee Ann's son-in-law or stepson?"

Jack shook his head, grinning, as he pushed his food around on his plate, thinking what an odd and wonderful problem that would have been. But he forced the thought aside and tried to focus on his next move. "I think I'll go get a haircut."

His grandfather put his fork down and stared at him. "So...you really are thinking of taking off?" When Jack didn't answer, the old man said, "Because you always get a haircut before you go off on one of your sabbaticals."

Jack tucked long strands of hair behind his ears. "Maybe."

Chapter Eleven

Addison hurried through her last appointment for the day, anxious to check on her mother. Mom didn't want to hire anyone else through the agency, and Addison had gone along with that, even though she was worried about her mother remembering to take her meds...and worried about her overall mental state.

"Look, look, look!" Mom jumped up and down like a toddler when Addison walked into the living room. "Read it. It's from Wil—I mean Oliver." She smiled as she pushed an envelope at Addison. "I'm going to have to get used to that, calling him Oliver. Read it."

Addison was glad to see her mother so happy, but cautious about sharing her mother's joy until she heard what *Oliver* had to say. And even then, she wasn't sure if she wanted her mother involved with someone like him. She pulled the letter from the envelope.

My Dearest Lee Ann,

I don't know what you've been told about my departure, but let me just say this—I've had four great loves in my life. The Lord, my beloved wife Claire, my grandson Jackson (Logan)...and now you. Yes, there were lies and betrayals. But please know that I wasn't lying when I said I love you.

Addison took a deep breath. *Jackson. His name is Jackson.* She kept reading.

Perhaps I shouldn't make excuses for what we did, but I guess I will anyway. I had cancer, Lee Ann, and while I was prepared to meet my Maker, I wasn't sure Jackson could handle another loss. He loved his grandmother very much. Claire and I raised Jackson (we're the only ones who call him that, others just call him Jack). He's a good boy. Or, I guess I should say, he is a good man. Although, I look at the man he's become, and it's mindboggling where all the time went.

I was in the United States (yes, I really was born in Surfside Beach, Texas) for cancer treatment. Things got complicated, and well...next thing you know, we were both being sent back to Australia. And I've been told we can't go back to the United States.

I'm asking you from the bottom of my heart to forgive this old man. I've enclosed a voucher for a round-trip ticket to Australia. Or just make it one way—that's what I'll be hoping for. My boy tells me our homeland is on your bucket list, anyway. Come to the Australian Outback and let an old guy show you around. He'd be willing to love you till the end of time if you'd have him. Have I mentioned that I love you?

Addison couldn't help but smile, but she wondered how he could afford such a gift since she'd gotten the impression that neither Logan—Jack—or Oliver had much money. She glanced at her mother, whose face glowed like a new bride, blissfully happy and hopeful for the future. Addison knew her mother had forgiven Oliver before she even read the letter.

I'm happy to purchase a ticket for Addison to accompany you here if you are uncomfortable traveling by yourself. I'd be happy to do this, and of course, I'd be delighted to see her as well.

Addison swallowed back the sob that threatened to escape, determined not to ruin this moment for her mother. But not even a mention about Jack, if he missed her or thought about her, or anything. Maybe she'd misread the unspoken signals between them. Or maybe that's why he'd never kissed her.

So, my love, I'm including my phone number at the end of this letter, in hopes to hear your voice soon. If not, I'll understand. But just know, I don't have any regrets. If things had turned out any differently, I wouldn't have been led to you.

My love always,

Oliver Lloyd Easten

Addison fought the disappointment that cocooned her, an ending that never really had a defined beginning. But what did she expect? She handed the letter back to her mother.

"I'm happy for you, Mom. I really am." She smiled, genuinely, as it warmed her heart to see such joy from her mother. "You deserve this, and I guess I don't even have to ask if you're going."

Her mother grabbed both her hands, still clutching tightly to the letter. "Come with me, Addie."

Addison shook her head. "No, Mom. I wasn't invited."

"Of course you were! Didn't you read the part about Oliver getting you a ticket too?"

Addison sighed. "No, Mom. That's not what I mean. Jack didn't invite me, and I haven't heard from him. It would be awkward to just show up. If he wanted to see me, he would have called or written. Clearly, his feelings for me weren't the same as Oliver's are for you." She hugged her mom, then eased away. "I am very happy for you, if not a bit worried. How well do you know this man? Well enough to fly across the world to visit him?"

Her mother cupped her cheeks. "Yes, and you're going to have to trust on me this. And I'm going. I've already called him, and I'm leaving Thursday. We're old, Addie." Mom clapped her hands together. "No time to waste."

Addison knew her eyes were bulging. "Already? I mean, that's in three days. Don't you have to get things in order, pack, take care of things? What about a passport?"

Mom waved an arm around the empty room. "I've done everything. I got a passport months ago when I knew I would be traveling someday. And if I choose to come back, I already have a reserved spot at the assisted living facility. But Addie...I'm not ready to just be an old lady who travels from time to time. I want to *live*, to be loved."

"You will call me every step of the way, right? And you'll remember to take your meds too, right?"

Mom nodded, grinning. "And I won't talk to strangers either."

Addison smiled, as her mother brought two hands and the letter she was still clutching to her chest. "Addie, this letter just came today. Have you been home yet?"

Addison shook her head. "I came straight from my last showing. Why?"

Mom turned her around and almost pushed her out the door. "Scoot! You might have a letter waiting at your house too!"

"I doubt it." But suddenly, she was anxious to get home.

Jack listened as his grandfather detailed Lee Ann's travel plans for Thursday. "I'm happy for you, Grandpa. I really am." He wished more than anything that Addison was coming, but his grandfather had offered to buy her a ticket, and there'd been no interest on her end. He was pretty sure he'd misread her.

"I still think you should phone Addison. It's not too late."

Jack slouched into the couch and crossed an ankle over his knee and shrugged.

"You haven't gotten a haircut yet, so you must not be ready to hit the road." His grandfather chuckled.

"I have an appointment to get it cut this afternoon."

"Then what?" Grandpa folded his arms across his chest.

"I don't know yet."

His grandfather sat down beside him. "Take some time to get out of your head, as you put it. You've certainly got the money to do so since we couldn't get to our money for two years. I'm proud of the way you worked so hard in the States to take care of both of us when things got so messed up and you could no longer be Jackson Easten the accountant or engineer. I know home health care wasn't your career choice."

Jack shrugged. "It wasn't so bad. I met a lot of nice people. Besides, it was all Logan Northrupp was qualified to do."

"Maybe when you get back, you'll decide to go back into accounting or engineering. Although, I gotta say, neither of those seemed suited to you. Maybe go to culinary school! The world is wide open to you, Jackson. Choose your path, and if it feels right, it's the right one."

Jack nodded. Even though he wasn't sure anything was going to feel right without Addison.

Addison didn't even shut the car door as she darted to the mailbox in front of her house. She yanked the lid down, grabbed the mail, and rushed through the three envelopes. Not a one of them from Jack. Tucking the mail under her arm, she stopped at her car to get her purse, slammed the door shut, and marched to her front door. She turned the key in the lock, but heard someone honking, so she glanced over her shoulder and gasped.

Connor? She stood perfectly still as he swaggered toward her never looking better in a pair of khaki shorts and a yellow Polo shirt. His dark hair was neatly parted to one side, and he was sporting a dark tan to go with the new Corvette he'd apparently bought since they'd broken up.

"Nice car," she said softly, glancing around him at the black Vette. "What are you doing here?" She quickly calculated that she hadn't laid eyes on him in almost eight months, and that had been a chance meeting at Starbucks. An awkward moment with him and Mandy…the girl he'd cheated with, glued to his side, blinking long, fake eyelashes at Addison.

He kept walking until he was right in front of her. "Mandy and I broke up." He hung his head, then looked back up at her. "And it's just as well. She knows I've always been in love with you."

Addison stared at him "Who ended it? You or her?"

"She did. But Addison—" He reached for her arm and she pulled away.

"I'm not your consolation prize, Connor. I'm no one's second choice."

"Baby, you've always been my first choice. Always." His eyes watered up as he moved closer again, but Addison put an arm out.

"No, Connor. You can't come here just because your heart has been trampled on, then expect me to welcome you back with open arms. It doesn't work like that."

"I know that. I'm just asking for another chance. Doesn't a guy deserve a second chance?"

Addison lowered her arm and stared at the man she'd been ready to marry, to build a life with. And here he was, offering to make that dream a reality.

"You cheated on me. For months."

He hung his head again, and a tear rolled down his cheek. "I know. And I've never been sorrier. Please, babe. Let's give it another try."

At that very moment, Addison knew that she should feel some sort of hope for the future. But the only thing that came to her mind was Logan. *Jack.* She searched her mind in an effort to recall one conversation that she'd ever had with Connor about God, faith, love, loss, or anything that wasn't a shallow conversation about the materialistic things they both wanted down the line. Jack probably didn't have a dime to his name, but he'd shown her the way back to God and guided her onto a path of spirituality. She liked where she was in that regard.

But as she recalled the fond memories of Jack, she reminded herself that he hadn't tried to contact her in any way. She was easy to find on the Internet via the company she worked for, Facebook, and several other public profiles. She'd never even shared a kiss with Jack. And yet, with Connor, she'd planned an entire future, lending weight to the fact that maybe Connor did deserve another chance.

"I'll think about it," she finally said to Connor.

"I'll spend the rest of my life making this up to you, Addison. I swear." He moved closer, but again, she kept him at arm's distance.

"I said, I'll think about it."

He took an exaggerated step backward, nodding. "That's all I can ask." He kept walking backward until he was at his car. "I'll call you later."

"Okay," she said and she watched him drive down the street, keeping her eyes on his car until he was around the corner and out of sight.

Later, after a shower, she spread the familiar pile of pictures on her bed, but for the first time in a year, she didn't feel like throwing them on the floor and stomping on them. She picked up each photo, recalling where they had been when the picture was taken, soaking in some of the happiest memories of her life.

By the time the phone rang later that evening…Addison had made her decision.

Chapter Twelve

Jack was thankful that he and his grandfather lived close enough to Jervis Bay to walk there. He needed to get an early start before the weekenders started arriving and the winds picked up in the afternoon. He made his way to the Greenfield Beach picnic area, south of Vincentia, to start the White Sands Walk. As he looked out over deep blue water, he dug his toes into what was recognized by the Guinness Book of Records as the whitest sand in the world. A far cry from the beaches on Galveston Island. But he felt like he'd left a part of himself back in Texas.

As he hugged the water's edge, he pulled his phone from his pocket. Addison's number had been easy enough to find, but every time he opened her contact page on the phone, he hit End. So, instead, he'd just stare at the picture that he'd attached to her profile, a photo from the real estate agency's website.

Was it real, what he'd felt for her? And did she feel anything for him? He'd intentionally avoided kissing her, and even though he regretted it on one level, he was relieved on another level, unsure if his heart could have taken the separation.

He'd been in love one other time in his life, right before he'd left for the United States. There'd been all kinds of promises made, but the distance between continents had not made their hearts grow fonder.

He picked up the pace and hoped he'd spot a kangaroo today. Or maybe a dolphin. Either way, his trek would take him through a chain of pristine beaches, through the bush track, and some of the most gorgeous rock formations on the planet. A good place to clear a guy's head. His backpack was in the car, and once he'd stabilized his thoughts, he'd figure out which way to head. He was just glad to be out of the house before Lee Ann arrived, due there any minute. And it was an opportunity to visit his favorite place in the world.

Addison stood beside her mother, in awe of her surroundings. Oliver and Jack's house wasn't right on the beach, but you could see the ocean from the wraparound porch that enclosed the entire house, which was painted a light shade of blue and set against white stone. Calburra Beach, population 3,500, looked like the setting for a postcard. Oliver had shared with her mother that a trusted friend had paid the bills and kept the place up while Oliver and Jack were in the United States.

"I'm so glad you decided to come with me at the last minute." Mom was glowing like a schoolgirl on her first date with two large red suitcases beside her. Addison had packed so hurriedly, she only had a carry-on, and she was sure she'd forgotten some things. Not to mention, she had gotten a look at herself in the mirror at the airport bathroom and she was far from glowing. She'd never been one to sleep much on a plane, and jet lag hung beneath her eyes in dark circles. She glanced again at her mother and didn't think she'd ever looked more beautiful.

Her mother knocked on the door with shaky hands. Oliver had insisted on picking them up at the airport, despite the fact that he would have to reschedule a doctor's appointment. But Mom had argued that he needed to keep the appointment and that she and Addison would take a cab. Addison's mother had won that argument, and Addison suspected Oliver would give in to her mother's every whim. She'd been concerned about the recent hiccups in his life and if her mother would be okay here, but seeing her mother this happy made it seem worth any risk.

"I just assumed...that they...lived modestly." Addison glanced around at the pristine houses, exquisite flowers and greenery, and shops in the distance. Touristy, but quaint. "They're rich."

"I wouldn't care if Oliver lived in a hut," her mother said, a permanent smile fixed on her face. And in reality, Addison had been prepared to stay in a homestead of modest means, and she hadn't cared either if it was a hut. But the thought of spending the night under the same roof as Jack caused her heart to skip a beat. The four of them had spent so much time together over the past few weeks, it would almost seem like a reunion, but she wondered how Jack would react when he saw her.

Addison had shown up at the airport with hopes she could get a ticket on her mother's flight. She'd packed, met Connor for coffee, given him the news that there would be no second chance for them, then zoomed to the airport. She knew she'd never forget the look on her mother's face when Addison came down the aisle of the plane. And if things didn't go well with Jack, there would be no regrets. It was a mother-daughter trip—and this was a second chance she wasn't going to miss.

As the breeze swirled around them on Oliver and Jack's porch, the door finally opened. Oliver blinked his eyes a few times. "You are early. A gift from God." He rushed into Lee Ann's arms, and Addison knew she was blushing as the couple smothered each other in kisses right there on the porch. She tried to look past Oliver, to see if Jack was lingering behind him, but all she saw was a wide open space decorated with colorful wicker furniture, brightly lit, and a bird chirping in the background.

"That's Heidi our budgie, similar to what you'd call a parakeet," Oliver said as he eased away from Lee Ann, then moved toward Addison. "What a wonderful surprise. But shame on you for not allowing me to buy you a ticket." He kissed Addison on the cheek before pulling her into a hug.

"It was a last minute decision," Addison said, still trying to see over his shoulder in hopes that Jack was home.

"Come in, come in. Jack prepared some appetizers before he left, and I have tea or coffee ready."

Mom began to question Oliver about his doctor's visit, but all Addison heard was *before he left*. Of course, he would be at work. Why hadn't she thought of that? But would he have a job so soon? Maybe he was running errands. Most likely, he wanted to give his grandfather and Addison's mother time alone, so he'd made himself scarce for a while, since he didn't know Addison was coming. Or would he have made himself scarce had he known she was coming? Finally, she couldn't stand it anymore.

"Is Jack here?" she asked above their conversation.

Oliver let out a heavy sigh, and Addison's stomach flipped as she swallowed hard.

"My dear Addison. I wish we would have known you were coming. Jack is a responsible, loving grandson. But from time to time he ventures off the beaten path to clear his head. And this time, I think perhaps his heart was involved." Oliver touched her gently on the arm. "I'm afraid Jack left about an hour ago."

"Oh." She forced a smile. "Will he be back soon?" Suddenly, she was more anxious than ever to tell him how she felt. She'd wasted too much time in her life wishing it away. She was going to live her life, like her mother planned to do. And the first thing on the agenda was to tell Jack how she felt. If he rejected her, she'd treat this as a nice vacation, then go home. Maybe it was all the kissy-face she'd witnessed with her mother and Oliver, but the moment she saw Jack, she was going to smother him in affection too.

"I don't know when Jack will be back, Addison."

Oliver's words stung like a hundred bees. "Um…what?"

"Sit down." He motioned them to a colorful couch that faced a plush garden on the other side of a plate glass window. Heidi was enjoying the sunshine from a large cage on the patio, vocalizing the intrusion. Once they were seated, Oliver went on. "I might not hear from Jack for days or even weeks. From time to time, Jack ventures out on a bit of a spiritual journey. Although…" He tapped a finger to his chin. "I think there is probably surfing involved."

Addison tried to smile, unsuccessfully. She'd been right, though, pegging him as a lifeguard or someone with a love of the water, with his golden tan, strong arms, and long blond hair.

"Anyway, whenever I do hear from him, he will be devastated that he missed you. I think that's part of the reason he went to 'get out of his head' as he calls it. I think it's his heart he's trying to run from. And we all know there's no escaping our feelings."

Addison's emotions merged. "Feelings for me?" she said in a meek voice, hoping she hadn't misunderstood.

Oliver smiled. "Of course, dear girl. The boy is in love with you. But he is convinced you could never forgive him for the lies." He glanced at Lee Ann. "I've been on bended knees daily, thanking God that you chose to forgive me." He reached for her hand before turning back to Addison. "How long can you stay?"

Addison took in the image of her mother and Oliver, possibly the cutest couple she'd ever seen. "I don't know for sure."

"I have the guest bedroom ready for your mother, and I could have the other extra bedroom down the hall ready with little effort. I'd just have to clear some of Jack's painting supplies out of there. He's really very good. I've encouraged him to show some of his work at a local gallery, but he says it's just a hobby."

"I had no idea he painted." Addison realized she didn't know much at all about Jack. Maybe this trip hadn't been a good idea. As she eyed her mother and Oliver, she could see that the girl trip part of this adventure was coming to an end.

"I'll probably just wander around and see some of the nearby sights, then go home in a few days. But don't go to any extra trouble, I can stay in Mom's room with her."

"Absolutely." Mom smiled at Addison, but Addison could see her own hurt reflected in her mother's eyes. "We will have a wonderful time while you're here. And maybe Jack will check in during that time."

"Maybe," she whispered, swallowing back tears.

Jack wiped sweat from his forehead, thankful he'd cut his hair. Even if he did look like an engineer now, a job he'd get to someday, just not anytime soon. When the time was right, he'd design his own home near Jervis Beach, with a view of the ocean. The only thing that would be missing would be Addison. He wondered if he'd made a mistake by not calling her, and he tried to envision the Addison he'd left, the one who'd become more trusting, the girl who smiled more. The woman who'd reestablished her relationship with God. He pulled his phone from his pocket, pulled off his sunglasses, and pulled up her profile again. What did he have to lose? *Just call her.* But he stuffed the phone back in his pocket, knowing he'd given her another reason not to trust the men in her life.

When he reached the entrance to the White Sands Walk, he chugged some water, put his shades back on, and prepared to walk the hour-long loop down the bush track to Hyams Beach. It would be his best chance to spot a kangaroo or some of the more colorful birds in the area. He'd keep his hand on his phone in case a photo op presented itself, but he also needed to give some thought to where he might go after this. He was about three hours south of Sydney, but the big city had no allure for him. Getting out of his head required reliance on God, the beauty of his surroundings, and mental clarity. When he got home, he'd make some plans to put together a life for himself. He slowed his pace to take time for prayer.

Addison decided to give her mother and Oliver some time alone. She suspected they had a future to plan. Addison tried to envision her mother living here, so far away. But she was resolved to support whatever choices her mother made.

When she reached the beach, she slipped off her flip-flops and tucked them in the pocket of her white cargo shorts, thankful for the loose pink shirt she'd chosen. Her outfit reminded her of her day at the beach with Logan. *Jack, Jack, Jack*. She was still getting use to that. *Jack Easten*. She'd been wearing pink and white that day too.

She was sure this was the whitest sand she'd ever seen, and she'd known the water would outshine Galveston by a mile, but it was even bluer than she could have imagined. Watching two sailboats in the distance, she wondered if she'd have a job when she got back. She'd been there for a long time, but her boss hadn't taken kindly to her giving one-day notice that she was leaving and no firm date of when she'd be back. She was missing three closings this week that would fall on Sandra. But something deep inside of her knew that she'd never have peace until she found out if there was something real going on with her and Jack. It felt genuine to her, but she reminded herself that he hadn't made contact.

When she saw the entrance to the White Sands Walk to Hyams Beach, she recalled Jack's comment about going there the first Friday of each month. She stopped in her tracks, the wind tossing her hair across her face. She'd realized on the plane that today was the first Friday of the month. A sign from God or a coincidence?

She stood perfectly still, staring at the sign to the entrance. Oliver had made Jack's trip sound more like a sabbatical, not a trek in familiar territory not far from where he lived. But she did want to see the place Jack found special enough to walk it once a month for most of his life, minus the past seven years.

She made the turn on the trail, and within a few minutes, she could see the allure and thanked God for leading her to this place. She could almost feel Jack nearby, and it was easy to picture him getting lost in thought amidst the soothing coos from nearby birds, mixed with a gentle breeze. Taking her time to absorb her surroundings and chat with God, she rounded the corner…and had the shock of her life.

Standing in front her, tall and fierce, was a huge kangaroo. And as he moved toward her, it become clear…this large fellow was not happy.

Chapter Thirteen

Jack ran a hand through his much shorter hair and wondered if Addison would like it this length. Was this how it would always be? Constant thoughts about the Texas girl he'd been forced to leave behind. He rounded the corner, and at first glance, he was excited to get his wish. A kangaroo with his back to him was farther down the trail. But when he got closer, he could see a woman in the distance. He hoped it was a local who knew what to do when facing a kangaroo, and not a tourist.

He picked up his pace, and right away, he knew the woman wasn't from here. She was taking steps backward away from the kangaroo. Locals knew to turn to the side and avoid eye contact. A kangaroo that size could slice open a person's abdomen with its sharp claws. One kick could crush a person's insides. It was rare to see one this time of day. Normally, you'd only catch a glimpse of a buck this size in the early morning hours or twilight.

"Hey!" Jack called out to try to get the animal's attention. He'd bet money that the woman had food in her pockets. Otherwise, a buck like that would have just taken off. But the tourists had made a habit of trying to feed the kangaroos, despite the warnings, and the animals had become more comfortable getting close to people. "Hey!" he yelled again as he got closer. "If you have any food in your pocket, toss it to the side!" He tried to peek around the animal to see if she heard, but all he saw was something fly to her left. *Must have been food.* The animal scurried toward the tossed item, then hopped away.

Jack put a hand to his forehead as he drew closer, and what he saw almost dropped him to his knees.

"Addison…" He could barely speak as his heart thudded in his chest. He glanced around, then back at her, to make sure she was real.

Addison smiled, tempted to run into his arms like she'd envisioned, but the thought that he'd never called or written returned to the forefront of her mind like a roadblock she couldn't get past. "Hi Lo— *Jack.*"

His jaw hung low as he slowly walked toward her. She hadn't recognized him at first with his short haircut. "What are you doing here?" A smile filled his face as he stopped a foot from her.

"Someone who frequents this place saved me from a big kangaroo that wanted my energy bar." She shrugged, trying to look casual. "First Friday of the month. I took a chance." Forcing a smile, she trembled, despite the heat swirling in the breeze. "Nice haircut."

Jack was still smiling. "What are you doing here?" he asked again. "Grandpa said he offered to buy you a ticket, but he said you weren't coming."

"It was a last-minute decision." She considered telling him that she didn't want her mother traveling alone, but that wouldn't be true, and one thing she wanted above all else right now was honesty. "I wanted to see you," she said almost in a whisper.

"On a normal First Friday, I would have already walked this loop. I was late leaving today. I helped Grandpa make some snacks to have for your mum when she got here." He paused, shook his head. "What are the chances that I'd run into you before I took off on my trip?"

She took a deep breath and reminded herself that she couldn't expect Jack to change plans he'd made just because she showed up. But at the very least, she wanted to know how things stood. "Where are you headed?"

He laughed. "I have no idea!" His expression grew serious. "I guess I was running…anywhere…somewhere, to clear my head and see if it would help my heart." He gently pounded his chest with one fist.

"What—what's the problem with you heart?"

He hung his head for a few moments before he looked back up at her and locked eyes. "There's this girl…woman." He waited for a reaction, but Addison wasn't breathing. "She is what's wrong with my heart. I was falling for her while I was pretending to be someone else. But I can't help but wonder if she has similar feelings for me."

"Ah…so you lied to her," she said, keeping her eyes on his.

"I did. My intentions were good, but I was pretty sure this woman wouldn't forgive me for the lies. The last two men in her life that she was close to betrayed her, and I didn't think she'd see past my lies to understand why I did what I did."

She pressed her lips together, trying to play it straight and cool, but all she could focus on was Jack saying he'd fallen for her. "What if—what if…this woman understood your motives, but she didn't understand why you didn't call or write."

Jack latched onto both her shoulders. "I would tell her that I didn't want to cause her more pain. I've missed you, Addison, and I don't think it's a coincidence that you're here. I thought I saw something in your eyes, too, something real, and I—"

She cupped his cheek in her hand, leaned up, and pressed her mouth to his, lingering there for a long while. She was pretty sure she heard angels singing in the distance. When she finally eased away from him, what she saw was a kind man, someone who loved his grandfather, and who had been very good to her mother. A man who'd shown Addison a way back to God.

"Now, we've kissed," she whispered. "What now?"

Jack let out a long breath. Would he leave on his sabbatical? Would she hear from him again? What did the future hold with Jack in Australia and her life in the United States?

"We don't have to figure everything out this very minute." He pushed a strand of hair from her face. "But...I need to know...need to know if..." He sighed. "I regret the way I've handled things, and I'm having trouble forgiving myself for lying to you. To God. I just need to know if—"

"If I have feelings for you?"

He nodded, keeping his gaze on hers. "Yes. I'll accept whatever answer you give me. I just need to know."

She latched on to his hand and gently pulled. "Let's take a walk." He squeezed her hand, and she squeezed back. "Someone once told me that regrets will feed on you like a hungry predator, leaving you raw and unable to forgive yourself."

They were quiet for a while. Only the birds were having a conversation. But she figured she'd kept him on the line long enough. She slowed down, turned to him, and said, "My feelings for you are real. Real enough to come all the way here to see how you felt about me."

He wrapped his arms around her, kissed her on the forehead, and held her tightly. She held her head against his chest, against the beat of his heart, and wondered what the future held. Especially, the next few minutes. Would he still feel the need to leave, or was he done running?

After a few moments, they started walking again, but Addison couldn't shake the feeling that Jack had more on his mind. At the next inlet, the beach came into view, and he guided her off the path, and once they were in the sand, they moved toward the water. At the water's edge, Jack turned to her.

"Addison, I can't ask you to give up your life."

She choked back the knot forming in her throat and wondered if this was the part where he told her he was still leaving. He sat down in the sand, and she did the same, deciding to avoid his comment, afraid she might cry.

"This is the prettiest beach I've ever seen." She stared out at the deepest part of the ocean, where the royal blue met with the horizon. "I bet you're glad to be back here."

He stared out at the water for a few moments, then twisted to face her. "The tides have turned, and we live on different continents now, but I want you in my life." He reached for her hand, and she smiled.

"Tides ebb and flow," she said softly. "Like life. Like relationships. But the lowest ebb is the turn of the tide, as Henry Wadsworth Longfellow would say."

"I believe this is a tide worth turning." Jack leaned over and kissed her.

Addison waited.

"How long can you stay?" He reached for her hand.

How long do you want me to stay? She shrugged, unsure how to answer. "I—I don't know."

He smiled, and Addison wanted to say *forever*.

"You up for a road trip?" Still smiling, he squeezed her hand.

"To where?" Not that it mattered.

Now it was Jack who shrugged. "Wherever the tide takes us."

Addison had never done anything in her life that hadn't been meticulously planned out. She wasn't even sure she'd brought the basics for this trip. And now, Jack wanted her to pick up and just leave, destination unknown. Yet, nothing had ever sounded better to her. God had lead her this far. She smiled and squeezed his hand.

"I think I'm long overdue for a road trip."

And when Jack's lips met hers, she knew that she'd reached the place she wanted to be. With Jack.

Acknowledgments

It takes a group of dedicated people to grasp an idea, then mold it into an entertaining story. I'm blessed to have various teams for my projects.

My idea for A *Tide Worth Turning* was followed up with great editing, so much thanks goes to Natalie Hanemann.

To our team leader on this project—Janet Murphy—you continue to rock, and you are, indeed, irreplaceable. Thank you for everything. xo

Thank you to my BFF Renee' Bissmeyer and to my mother, Pat Isley, for speedily proofing the manuscript so we could meet the publishing deadline. Love you both always and forever.

To *Wiseman's Warriors*, you are the best street team a gal could have. Thank you for your dedication to helping me spread the word about Beth Wiseman books.

And it's an honor to dedicate this novella to Jamie Foley, our newest team member. Jamie, you are a bright light in our world, a talented writer, market savvy, and ridiculously smart. It's a true joy to walk alongside you on your writing journey, and I am deeply appreciative that God sent you our way.

And last, but never least, my heartfelt thanks to God for continuing to bless me with stories to tell.

Message in a Bottle

A NOVELLA

BETH WISEMAN

To Audrey Wick

Prologue

Kyle stretched tape across another box, then lifted it from the floor and piled it on top of the others that he had ready to go.

"I can't believe all this stuff was stashed in this small room." Lexie lowered a stack of file folders into a box. "I don't think I had nearly this much in my dorm room." She grinned as she slung long brown hair over her shoulders. "And I'm a girl. We keep everything."

Kyle eyed the organized mess in the place he'd called home over the past four years. "Some of it probably needs to be trashed, but I'll take a closer look at everything once I get settled in my apartment." He handed Lexie the tape. "Just think, you'll be right downstairs from me. No curfews or rules. We can eat pizza at three in the morning, and we won't have to deal with crazy roommates."

Lexie closed the distance between them and pressed her soft lips gently against his. Kyle eased his arms around her and basked in the scent of her flowery perfume. The feel of her mouth on his was a welcome distraction. They'd briefly considered moving in together, but Kyle's Catholic upbringing kept him from choosing that option. They'd done the next best thing: rented apartments close to each other.

"Maybe we should take a break from packing," Kyle whispered in her ear, trailing kisses down her neck.

She wiggled out of his arms. "Behave. We've got to get this done. You've got to be out of here by the end of the day." She walked to the built-in drawers in Kyle's room and tugged the bottom one until it inched open. "Good grief. What is all this?"

Kyle shuffled across the floor in his socks until he was beside her and staring at the massive amount of pictures, ticket stubs, receipts, and other memorabilia crammed in the top drawer. Sighing, he thumbed his way through the first layer. "Keepsakes."

Lexie smiled as she picked up a picture. "Awe, look at you and Aiden. So handsome."

"My mom sent me that the first week I was here, along with a bunch of other pictures." Kyle recalled how homesick he was at that time. "I was probably seventeen in that picture. Aiden was sixteen."

"Baseball players, I see." Lexie brought the photo closer to her face. "You and your brother look a lot alike in this picture, but not so much in person." She reached for a ticket stub that was folded in half and straightened it. Kyle rolled his eyes as she burst out laughing. "Lady Gaga?"

Kyle shrugged as his mind flooded with memories. "Yeah, well. I wasn't the one who wanted to go see her, but she actually put on a great show."

"Was this your date?" Lexie held up a photo that was right underneath the ticket. Kyle had his arm around the first girl he'd ever loved. Morgan Calhoun. And thoughts of her still caused his heart to race, even though he was sure no one could be in love as much as he and Lexie. There was no doubt in his mind that he'd marry Lexie one day.

"Yeah. That's Morgan." He swallowed hard. "We grew up on the same street, our families went to the same church, and our moms were best friends." He forced a smile. "My first—and only love—before you."

"Kyle Brossmann, do you expect me to believe that there have only been two loves in your life?"

The question made Kyle wonder how many loves had been in Lexie's life, but it really didn't matter. He'd be the one blessed to live with her for the rest of his days. He hoped.

Kyle nodded. "Yep. There was Morgan. And now you." He eased the photo from her hand and studied Morgan's face, the way her blonde hair curled under slightly below her chin, then tapered past her shoulders. She had magnificent brown eyes and a smile that made people like her before she ever uttered a word. And a body that made guys go nuts. Kyle had questioned her interest in him from day one, knowing someone as attractive as Morgan could have dated anyone she wanted.

"She's really pretty. I'm surprised you haven't mentioned her before." Lexie put her head on his shoulder. "How long did you two date?"

Kyle tucked his dark hair behind his ears, knowing he'd have to shed his long locks before he started his new job. "We dated about a year, but we sort of grew into it. Since we'd known each other most of our lives, we were friends way before anything else." He set the picture back in the drawer, forcing thoughts of Morgan away. Five years later, it was still painful to think about her. But Lexie had already found another selfie of Morgan and Kyle at the beach, the murky Gulf of Mexico in the background. Kyle remembered the cloudy day in Galveston. They'd eaten at Shrimp 'N Stuff and walked on the beach. Kyle looked like his face was twice as big as it really was in the picture. But Morgan looked perfect in her pink bikini top and freshly applied lip gloss.

Lexie couldn't seem to pull her eyes away from the photo. That's the affect Morgan had on most people.

"So what happened with you two?"

It was a conversation Kyle didn't want to have, but if he was going to marry Lexie some day, he supposed there shouldn't be any secrets. "It's a crazy story."

Lexie nudged him gently with her elbow, grinning. "I love crazy stories."

Kyle took a deep breath as all the memories he'd fought to suppress came rushing to the surface. He lowered himself to the edge of the mattress, perching on the corner as he began. "Back in high school, I pulled up to Morgan's house in my truck and honked the horn. She rode with me to school every day, even though she had her own car. I waited, honked again, waited some more, then finally went to the front door and knocked. No answer." His heart hammered against his chest, but he figured he might as well get this over with, then he'd pack up his memories for good. Seal them tight with extra tape, keepsakes his grandchildren would find some day and ask, "Who is this woman grandpa is with?" From heaven, he'd whisper, "My first love."

"Then what?" Lexie eased her way to the bed and sat down.

"I looked in the window, and through the sheer drapes, I could see that the living room was empty. I mean, totally empty. No furniture. Nothing." Kyle felt the sweat beads pooling on his forehead, much like five years ago. "I opened the front door, which was unlocked, and I went through the whole house yelling Morgan's name." He turned to face Lexie, pushed the drawer shut with the heel of one foot, then leaned against the dresser. "There was not one piece of furniture in that entire house."

"I'm confused." Lexie tipped her head to one side, frowning. "Did Morgan and her family just pack up in the middle of the night and disappear?"

Kyle tried to calm the churning in his stomach. "That's exactly what happened."

"Where'd they go?"

"No one knows. It was totally bizarre. My mom was devastated. Maybe even more than me. Morgan's mom and my mom had been pregnant at the same time with us, and they'd been best friends long before Morgan or I could even walk. Mom even hired a private detective to try to find them, convinced that some sort of kidnapping or evil was at work. But the guy took Mom's money and never came up with one single clue."

"Wow." Lexie leaned back on the palms of her hands and blew out a big burst of air she'd been holding. "That *is* a crazy story. I bet that's really haunted you over the years."

You have no idea how much. "Yeah, it did." He walked to the bed, sat down beside her, and leaned in for a kiss. "But I have you. And wherever Morgan is, I hope she's well. But she's a part of my past. My future is with you."

But even as Kyle said the words, his thoughts and memories swam in his head like hungry sharks, wondering about Morgan. Where is she now? Is she happy? Did she go to college like they'd planned to do together?

Where are you, Morgan?

Chapter One

One year later…

Morgan sat in a chair by the hospital bed waiting for Emma to wake up. She always woke up, thank God. The medicines knocked her out, but she wasn't going to drift away in her sleep. Not today anyway.

"The guys left about three hours ago," her father said in a whisper as he walked into the room, gently closing the door behind him.

Morgan didn't turn around. She recognized her father well before she got a visual of him. Neal Calhoun had worn the same musky cologne Morgan's entire life. "I know."

She slumped into the chair as she watched her baby girl sleeping. Emma was five. Not really a baby. But curled in a fetal position on her side, and at six pounds lighter than when they'd arrived at the hospital, she looked like a tiny baby to Morgan.

Her father picked up a chair from the other side of the room and tiptoed to where Morgan was. He gently set the chair down and eased into it. "How's our girl today?"

"She's good." Morgan answered for her daughter since the medicine had made her drowsy. "The doctor was in earlier, and if she stays on this course the rest of the day, she can go home." Morgan reached for a cup of water on the nightstand.

Her father nodded to the lounging chair in the far corner. "Were you able to get some sleep during the night?"

Morgan finished sipping from the cup of water and put it back. "Yeah. As well as anyone can sleep in a hospital, I guess."

They were quiet for a few moments, both watching the rise and fall of Emma's chest as she slept. Morgan's dad crossed one leg over the other and gently kicked it into motion. Her father was a man trained not to show any sort of nervousness, but when it came to his daughter and granddaughter, he was as ineffective as a sheer curtain trying to block out ultraviolet rays.

She reached into her purse and pulled out a bottle of ibuprofen, popped two in her mouth, and chased them back with another swig of water. She stared into the almost empty bottle and thought about all the little notes she used to leave for Kyle on Fridays after school. It felt like a lifetime ago. He'd had an irregular heartbeat and took a pill for it every morning on the way to school after he had picked her up. After swallowing it without any water, he would toss the bottle in the console of his Chevy Silverado. On Fridays she'd sneak out to his truck and leave him a note inside the bottle, knowing he'd find it Saturday morning on the way to work. "Messages in a bottle" he'd tell her.

Emma coughed and both Morgan and her father watched and waited, but Emma stayed asleep. "She looks so much better," Morgan said to her father.

Dad shifted his weight in the chair, his foot still moving nervously back and forth. He finally uncrossed his legs, but he kept a slow steady tap of one shoe going. "Everything is going to be okay," he said softly.

Morgan was quiet for a few moments. "What if he doesn't come?"

"He'll come."

Dad was a man used to getting his way. He loved God and he loved his family, but his desire to protect and provide sometimes crossed so many lines that Morgan felt like she stayed on a tightrope, striving to maintain balance somehow.

"It's been almost six years. What if he's married? Gone? Doesn't care?" That last part didn't sound like Kyle, but people change. Morgan sure had.

She glanced at her father when she felt his gaze on her. She raised an eyebrow and reminded herself who she was dealing with. As a CIA agent, her father would know everything there is to know about Kyle.

"I told you, he's not married."

Morgan took a deep breath. "But you said he's planning on getting married."

"Not for a few months, according to my source."

Morgan's father never revealed his sources, and most of the time, Morgan was sure that was a blessing. Her heart grew heavy as she thought about Kyle marrying someone else. But then, why shouldn't he? Her family had surely knocked the breath from his lungs the day they'd packed up and left in the middle of the night. But her former love had obviously moved on and was planning a future with someone else. *As it should be.*

But oh…how she'd love to be a fly on the wall when Landon and Sean showed up at Kyle's door.

Kyle awoke to the smell of bacon sizzling and coffee brewing. He stretched, yawned, and sat up in bed, knowing Lexie was busy in his kitchen. She did that most Saturdays, used her key, snuck in, and started breakfast. She'd arranged the kitchen in Kyle's apartment the way she liked it, knowing it would be her kitchen in a few months. Kyle was ready. Lexie was the love of his life, everything he'd ever wanted in a spouse and soul mate.

"Good morning, sleepyhead." She walked into the bedroom and handed him a cup of coffee.

"You spoil me," he said before he took a sip.

"You deserve to be spoiled." Lexie sat down on the side of his bed, smiling, and in full makeup.

"Where are you off to so early?" Kyle ran a hand through his short hair, not more than a couple of inches on the top and closely shaved on each side.

"I'm picking up Mom, and we're heading to a little boutique on the other side of Houston." Lexie rolled her eyes, grinning. "I'm starting to wonder if she'll ever find a dress for the wedding." She nodded toward the opened bedroom door. "I made you breakfast, but I already ate so I can get on the road."

Lexie's parents lived about forty-five minutes from the complex where Kyle and Lexie each had an apartment. Soon, there would be a merger into just Kyle's apartment, and not only could Kyle not wait to wake up next to Lexie every morning, they'd also be able to sock away some money by having just one rent to pay.

She leaned down and kissed him, grimacing.

"You should know better than to do that before I brush my teeth." He set the cup down and pulled her to him anyway, smothering her with kisses as she faked a struggle.

"Ewe, yuck, mister." She giggled as she finally freed herself. "Get your lazy butt up and brush those teeth." Blowing him a kiss, she turned at the door of his bedroom when he said her name. "Yeah?"

Kyle sat up in bed and stared at her. He didn't think she'd changed at all over the two years since he'd first met her, except she'd grown even more beautiful, if that was possible. "Do you have any idea how much I love you?"

She playfully tapped a finger to her chin, lifting an eyebrow as she pushed long strands of hair away from her face. "Hmm... I believe you said you love me with all your heart."

Kyle smiled. *I am a blessed man.* "With all my heart, to the moon and back."

She blew him another kiss and left.

Kyle shuffled to the kitchen, ate two pancakes and some bacon, then decided more sleep was in order on this rainy Saturday. Houston was hot in June. Throw in some rain, and it was miserably muggy. He awoke an hour later when someone banged on the door.

"Coming!" He slipped into a pair of jeans he'd left on the floor the night before, and he pulled a black ZZ Top T-shirt over his head on the way to see who it was. Looking through the peep hole, he saw two tall—and large—men. One of the guys looked to be about Kyle's age or a little older, and he wore a dark suit. The other man was considerably older and wore tan slacks and a yellow Polo shirt. "Yeah, what is it?" he yelled through the door.

"Kyle Brossmann? We need to talk to you. Can we come in?" the older guy asked. When Kyle didn't answer, the same man held up a... *badge?* Kyle closed one eye and squinted with the other until he could read the small print. *Central Intelligence Agency.*

Kyle's heart thudded so hard against his chest he feared he might have a heart attack at his young age. Recently, he'd gotten a speeding ticket. He'd sped through the toll booth without paying too. He'd paid his Visa credit card two days late. He'd cut the tag off a new pillow even though it warned not to.

His head was reeling, but he couldn't think of anything to warrant the CIA at his door. *Lexie.* Had something happened to her? *But the CIA doesn't show up to report an accident.*

"Uh, what can I help you with?" he managed to say loudly.

"Mr. Brossmann, we just need a few minutes of your time. Can you open the door?" Now the young guy was talking, but while Kyle was still pondering what to do, the older man held his identification even closer to the peep hole.

These guys aren't going away. Kyle opened the door. "Yeah?"

"We're sorry to bother you so early, but it's important we talk to you," the older guy said.

Kyle glanced at his watch. It wasn't so early. Ten o'clock. But he held his position.

The younger of the two men cleared his throat. "We need to talk to you about Morgan Calhoun."

Kyle's heart pounded like a jack pump in an oilfield. "What about her? Is she hurt or something?" *Or dead.* Adrenaline coursed through his veins, winding and weaving and causing havoc at every nerve ending in his body. Why else would the CIA show up at your door unless there had been a death, a murder, or something equally as awful? He stepped aside so the men could come in, each one stowing an umbrella by the front door. "Where is she?" It was the question Kyle had put to rest years ago, deciding it was a mystery that would never be solved.

"Morgan's fine." The older man extended his hand. "I'm Sean, and this is Landon."

Morgan is okay. Relief washed over Kyle in a wave of emotion that threatened to knock him off his feet. He latched on to Sean's hand, wondering if these guys had last names, and hoping he would get some answers after all these years.

Sean pointed to the couch. "Can we sit and talk for a few minutes?"

Kyle nodded. He was pretty sure he wasn't supposed to argue with the CIA.

Sean and Landon sat on the couch. Kyle found the edge of a recliner nearby, although he sat straight and rigid, barely breathing. Sean had thinning gray hair and dark eyes. The other guy—Landon—had wavy blond hair, a dark tan, and blue eyes. But they had one thing in common. They were both huge. And not in a bad sort of way, but muscular and thick.

"Where's Morgan?" Kyle asked again.

Sean glanced at Landon, then back at Kyle. "This is going to be a little shocking, but… "

"What?" Kyle asked in barely a whisper, hoping they didn't see his bottom lip trembling like it had a mind of its own.

"It's really more about Emma," Landon said.

"Who's Emma?" A surge of panic—or paranoia—spiked the hairs on his arms. Maybe he shouldn't have been so quick to let these guys in. "Are you guys talking in code or what?"

The two men exchanged stern looks again before Sean spoke. "Emma is your daughter, and she's very ill. Morgan was pregnant when she left Texas. Emma is five. We need for you to come with us."

Kyle stopped breathing. When he finally forced a breath, he stood up with weak knees and paced, his blood pressure surely off the chart. "I don't have a child." He'd been intimate with Morgan one time, and they'd both agreed it wouldn't happen again, unless they were married. "There's some sort of mistake."

"I'm sure you have a lot of questions, and we'll be happy to answer them all on the plane."

"Plane?" Kyle was still trying to process the possibility he might have a child. A sick child.

"What's wrong with the little girl?" He wasn't ready to say 'my daughter' just yet. This seemed far-fetched.

"She has a medical condition called aplastic anemia and needs bone marrow stem cells... from you, if she's going to live."

"*What?*" Kyle's knees were so shaky he had to sit back down.

Sean and Landon exchanged glances again, and Landon cleared his throat. "Other options have been exhausted. Emma's team of doctors have searched the database for an exact match, but because of her rare AB-negative blood type, a match couldn't be found. The best option is a sibling, but Emma doesn't have a brother or sister. You, as her father, would be a half match, giving her the biggest chance of beating this."

Kyle held his head in his hands as thunderclaps followed bursts of light from outside the window. His mind was formulating questions faster than he could organize the thoughts into words.

"Morgan or her parents can't help Emma. You are the one with the rare blood type who might be able to save her." Landon's eyebrows narrowed into a frown.

Kyle had always known his blood type was rare, and he gave blood as often as he could, hoping to help someone who needed it, but he couldn't have predicted this in a thousand years. "I—I... " His temples throbbed as his hands grew clammy. He'd had an anxiety attack once in his life, when he was twelve and saw a little girl on a bike get hit by a car. This felt like the same thing as his thoughts clouded into a swirl of confusion. He let go of his head and looked at Landon, then at Sean. "My bone marrow will save her life?" *A daughter? I have a child? Emma?*

"You're the best hope she's got," Landon said as he stood up.

Sean stood up also, but Kyle stayed seated, unsure if his legs would keep him upright.

"Where is she?"

Sean took a step closer to where Kyle was sitting. "We can't tell you that, Kyle, until after we are on the plane."

"What?" He finally stood up and folded his arms across his chest, but the action was mostly to calm his churning stomach. Giving himself a few moments to corral his thoughts, he said, "Two strangers show up at my door and tell me that my high school girlfriend is the mother of a child I didn't know I had. Now you expect me to travel to an undisclosed location to try to save her life." He hung his head, shaking it before he looked back at them. "How soon would I leave? I'd need to talk to my fiancée, and… " He blew out a long, windy sigh. "Oh man. Lexie. I have to tell Lexie."

"You can't, Kyle," Landon said as his eyebrows furrowed. "We need to leave right now, and you can't tell anyone."

"Uh, you're crazy. I can't just pack a suitcase and walk out the door to go wherever with you. How do I even know you're telling the truth?"

Landon and Sean stared at him with blank expressions, then they exchanged looks—again. Kyle was tired of being the third wheel in a conversation that was keeping him the dark.

"We have to leave now," Landon said as a muscle flicked in his jaw. The guy's eyes were hooded like a hawk ready to swoop down on his prey.

Kyle swallowed hard.

And I'm the prey.

Chapter Two

Lexie used her fork to dig out the chicken salad from between two pieces of bread.

"The bread is the best part of the sandwich here." Mom took a large bite of her own chicken salad sandwich. Candace White was one of those women who ate whatever she wanted and never gained weight. Lexie—regrettably—didn't inherit that gene from her mother. She had to work at staying thin.

"I know, but I'm trying to be careful between now and September. I want to be able to fit into my dress." Lexie smiled. Just the thought of being Kyle's wife kept her joyful through just about anything, even watching her mother try on sixteen dresses, not choosing any of them prior to lunch.

"I still think you kids are awfully young to be getting married, but we love Kyle." Mom shrugged. "So, I guess the heart knows what the heart wants."

"Twenty-three isn't all that young. We've already finished college and have great teaching jobs. It's time to settle down, and we both want a family."

"Plenty of time for that too," her mother said as a frown filled her face. "Have you had *the talk* with Kyle?"

Lexie knew exactly what her mother was referring to, and easing into that conversation would hamper the day much more than the rain. "No. But I will." *Please let it go, Mom.*

"You will be a great mother," her mom said quickly, as if she was having the same thought as Lexie. "But one thing at a time." She took a sip of tea, then let out an exasperated breath. "Where in the world am I going to find a dress for this wedding?"

Lexie shook her head, grinning. "I don't know, Mom. But I do know that I can't wait to be Mrs. Kyle Brossmann." She glanced at her phone on the table next to her plate, wondering why she hadn't heard from Kyle. Lexie had sent him a text over an hour ago, but as rain pelted the metal roof of the café, Lexie suspected Kyle had gone back to bed. It seemed like a day for that, and she wished she were cuddled up with him. Just holding each other, snuggling. She was proud that she and Kyle had agreed not to have sex until after they were married. It was an option that was growing less and less popular among her friends, but Lexie wanted to do right in God's eyes. She was glad Kyle shared her thoughts about the matter, even though he'd admitted to one slip up with his first girlfriend.

Morgan held a cup of water for Emma as her daughter sucked from a straw. Emma had been cleared to go home hours ago, but as was always the case, they'd been waiting around for discharge papers, instructions for home care, prescriptions, and a hoard of other information that always accompanied these unplanned hospital visits.

"Is the man coming today?" Emma leaned her head against the pillow, and Morgan nodded as she set the cup down on the tray in front of her daughter. "The man that's going to help me get well?" she added.

"Yes, he is. Remember I told you that this man has the same type of blood that you do, so that's important." Morgan and her parents had agreed not to tell Emma that Kyle was her father. It didn't seem fair to introduce Emma to a second parent, then tear her away from him again. It seemed equally as unfair to Kyle, but Morgan would do whatever it took to save Emma.

Morgan's father had gotten word an hour ago that Sean and Landon were on their way to the airport with Kyle. She couldn't even imagine what Kyle must be feeling. Would he hate her for keeping such a secret? It had been the only way to ensure that Emma would be safe. *But still.*

She wanted to be happy that Kyle had found someone to share his life with. He deserved that. Morgan was afraid to completely commit to another man since the recovery over losing Kyle had been excruciating. But she'd had Emma to focus on after she was born, which slowly eased the pain until she had stopped thinking about Kyle much at all. Until Emma turned four. It was then that her daughter's features matured in a way that reminded Morgan of Kyle. They both had big blue eyes and exceptionally long eye lashes. Emma had a perfectly proportioned nose like Kyle. Morgan was thankful for that since her nose was a tiny bit pugged. Her heart smiled when she recalled the way Kyle used to tell her what a cute nose she had. So many memories.

Emma's mouth had also taken on the same shape as Kyle's, and like his, Emma's smile lit up her face, crooking up just barely on one side, not enough that most people would even notice.

"Do Nana and Papa know the man who's coming?" Emma gazed at Morgan with curious eyes, as if this might be the most important question she'd ask today.

"No, they don't." *Forgive me, God.* Morgan despised lying, especially to her own daughter. But

Morgan loved Emma enough to protect her. How could she tell her own daughter that they had been relocated because her grandfather's life and entire family were being threatened? Her father had said that was the only way to keep everyone safe, even Kyle. Morgan hoped to spare Emma the kind of life she'd had growing up, the same way she planned to guard her heart from the type of heartache leaving Kyle had caused.

Morgan had plenty of tantrums when they'd first arrived at their new home, but they were all futile, and like it or not, this was her life. As she gazed at her beautiful daughter, she thanked God daily for this precious gift. And she begged Him daily to heal Emma.

Morgan had beat herself up for a long time for sleeping with Kyle, just once, when they were seventeen. But now, as she looked at Emma, she knew this was all just part of God's plan, and He was never wrong.

If Kyle was a match for Emma—and she prayed he was—she wondered how her father was going to handle Kyle being so close to the place they called home. Not even her grandparents knew where they were. Her father, along with Sean and Landon, had been vague about the entire plan.

Kyle stepped out of the black limousine. He was able to count on one hand the other times he'd been in such a vehicle—senior prom, a wedding, and a couple of funerals. He felt numb as the driver peeled away, leaving him with Sean and Landon. He glanced at his one piece of luggage. A girly red suitcase that Lexie must have left at his apartment. At the time, he'd grabbed the first thing he found. But now, he felt silly.

"That's the plane?" Kyle gulped as he eyed the small craft that was going to take him to wherever he was going. He'd just assumed they would be on a commercial flight.

"It's our biggest jet. Seats eight. There's a bar onboard if you need something to calm your nerves."

Kyle stood there, still trying to absorb the fact that he had a five-year-old daughter, who was terminally ill unless Kyle's bone marrow was a match for her. He wasn't a drinker, but he was sure there wasn't enough booze on that plane to calm his nerves. "Do you have a picture of her, of Emma?" The sun blazed down on them as they stood on the hot, black asphalt a few yards from the plane.

Sean shook his head, but Landon spoke up. "I do." He reached into his back pocket and took a photo out of his wallet. "Isn't she a beauty?"

Kyle had no words as he eyed the bright eyed, blonde girl in the picture. "She's beautiful," he finally said in a whisper before he offered the picture back to Landon.

"Keep it," he said, smiling.

Kyle turned his attention toward a plane that would carry him to California. "How long will I be gone?" Thankfully, he was a teacher and it was summertime. At least he didn't have his job to contend with.

"We're not sure." Sean waved to a pilot standing on the steps to the plane.

"I—I gotta call my fiancée and tell her what's going on." He'd gone this long without calling Lexie at Sean and Landon's insistence, but he couldn't get on a plane without at least telling her he was okay. "And I won't tell her where I'm going." *Not yet.* He hadn't been able to get a signal in the limo, which seemed odd. He pulled his cell phone from his pocket, but he couldn't get a call to go through.

Sean cleared his throat. "Your phone's been disabled and the service shut off."

"Say what?" The hairs on the back of Kyle's neck bristled. "Why?"

"From this point on, you can't have contact with anyone, not even Lexie. Not your mother, your grandparents, no one," Landon said.

"No deal." Kyle shook his head. "I'm not getting on a plane with two guys I don't know without telling someone what's going on."

"Those are the terms, and by being here with us, you've agreed." Sean shrugged. "We're not kidnapping you, Kyle. You can choose not to go. But if you do go, those are the rules. No contact with anyone until you return."

"What's to keep me from telling Lexie and everyone where I was when I get back?" He grunted, grinning. "Unless you're planning to just kill me after I help Emma."

Sean and Landon glanced at each other before Sean smiled. "I assure you, Kyle, no one is going to kill you."

"Well, forgive me, but you guys don't sound very convincing." Kyle folded his arms across his chest. "So... when I go missing, Lexie is going to report it. Then everyone is going to be wondering what happened to me, causing tons of grief for my family, and probably for you. Wouldn't it be better to avoid all of that and just let me call her right now?"

"Once you're on the plane, an email will be sent to Lexie from your email account, explaining to her that you need some time to think about things, about your relationship and whether or not marriage is the right step to take."

Kyle laughed. "Yeah, well, she'll never believe that. If anything, I'm the one who pushed her to get married. That's not going to fly. Our love is stronger than that, and she'll know that's not true."

"Maybe. Maybe not. But it will keep the authorities from looking for you and buy us some time." Landon nodded toward the plane. "We've got to go."

Kyle shook his head, but got in step with him on his way to the plane. "Where in California are we going?"

"LAX. Los Angeles," Sean said.

"I might need that drink after all." One thing he knew for sure… he'd find a way to contact Lexie when he got there. He was savvy enough to avoid these guys long enough to do that. So he decided to settle back and try to relax.

He was still holding the picture of Emma when the pilot started to taxi on the runway of the small, private airport. Landon and Sean were chatting with the pilot about the flight path, and just by overhearing, Kyle learned that both Landon and Sean were pilots also. That should have made him feel a little safe, but when Landon turned to pour himself a drink at the small bar to their left, Kyle saw a holstered gun.

Looking at the picture, his emotions swirled and collided, but he couldn't have lived with himself if he didn't make this trip in an effort to save Emma. *My daughter.*

Chapter Three

Morgan waited at the airport for Landon and Sean to arrive with Kyle. It was almost nine at night, but she felt at peace about Emma for now. Her daughter was home in her bed with her grandparents keeping a watchful eye on her. Morgan wondered if there would ever be a time in her life that she wasn't consumed with worry about Emma. So many times she'd tried to let go and let God, as her mother often said, but so many trips to the hospital ER kept Morgan teetering on the edge when it came to her faith. *Why can't God just make her well?*

Even though her relationship with God was on a slippery slope, she silently prayed that Kyle would be a match for Emma.

Morgan glanced at the time on her cell phone. She'd already calculated and allowed for the time changes going from Texas to California… and finally here. She wondered if Kyle knew where his final destination would be and if he'd ever been here before. As she glanced around the airport, she doubted it, unless he'd been here since she'd seen him, which was certainly possible. She suspected that Kyle's entire stay would be in the big city. She couldn't imagine her father allowing him to see where they live—on an island so private it's referred to as the 'forbidden island' by the locals.

She heaved her purse on her shoulder and looked at her cell phone again. The flight would take longer than a commercial flight, but the weather and direction of the wind could influence their arrival time by as much as an hour.

Morgan's stomach twisted in knots as she paced. She didn't think she looked much different than when Kyle last saw her, and she wondered if he'd changed. After Emma was born, it had taken a while to get rid of her baby weight, but she'd eventually lost it all and had remained about the same weight for the past four years. She fingered a strand of hair and pulled it in front of her. It was a lighter shade of blonde from all of her time in the sun, and living near a beach provided a year-round tan. There were some perks to living in a tropical paradise.

Morgan wondered what Kyle's fiancée looked like. Her father, along with Sean and Landon, knew everything there was to know about the woman— Lexie White. Morgan had the best luck getting information from Landon, but when she'd asked him about Lexie, Landon had just shrugged. "She's cute, I guess." Morgan had tried to push for more, but Landon had swerved his way out of the conversation, something Morgan suspected they taught at CIA school. Along with all kinds of other tactics that Morgan wasn't privy to.

She was surprised that her dad hadn't opted to come to the airport. Despite her father's job and ability to detach from his emotions when necessary, Neil Calhoun had loved Kyle for a long time. Morgan knew how hard this was for her. But it had to be difficult for her parents too. *So many memories.*

Kyle sat across from Landon, a small table in between them. Sean was in a nearby seat pounding away on a laptop.

"Are you going to eat that?" Landon nodded at Kyle's barely eaten sandwich and chips. He shook his head, pretty sure he'd vomit if he ate any more. He reached into his pocket and took out his bottle of pills, glad he'd remembered to grab his meds in all the commotion. Missing a dose for his heart condition wouldn't be the end of his world, but he would feel like his heart was somersaulting in his chest, more than it already was. He popped the Propranolol in his mouth.

His mind was awhirl with questions, but getting answers from Landon or Sean was like squeezing blood from a turnip. He spent a few minutes trying to organize his thoughts, then cleared his throat.

"Will Morgan be at the airport when we land in Los Angeles?" Kyle's heart fluttered at the thought of seeing her again, which made him feel a little guilty. He was in love with Lexie, and he didn't foresee Morgan changing his feelings about that. But somehow, picturing her raising their child was having a weird affect on him he couldn't identify.

Landon swiped at his mouth with a napkin, shaking his head. "No. She won't be in Los Angeles."

Kyle looked over at Sean, wondering if the older man would add anything, but he was sleeping, his head laid back against the seat and his laptop still open.

"Will she be in the vicinity when we land?" Kyle didn't try to keep the cynicism out of his voice.

"No." Landon stuffed a chip in his mouth. "But you'll see her. Eventually."

Kyle folded his arms across his chest and stared at the guy, tempted to ask Landon how old he was and how he'd landed a job with the CIA. He didn't look the part, aside from his athletic build. He had pretty-boy blond hair and not even a hint of five o'clock shadow. Nothing rough around the edges to signify he'd ever suffered more than a bad night's sleep. Kyle touched the scar on his chin, a foul ball that landed him six stitches. But even though Landon's job interested Kyle, it was far down the list.

"So …" Kyle waited until Landon ate the last chip on the plate and met eyes with him. "Is Morgan's dad in some kind of trouble? Is that why they moved in the middle of the night? Or is he in some sort of witness protection program?" Landon stared blankly at him. "Does it really matter if I know at this point?" Kyle briefly thought about his comment he'd made earlier, joking about whether or not these two men might kill him. He couldn't imagine Morgan's father would let that happen. Neal Calhoun had been the closest thing to a father Kyle had after his own father died. But then, he wouldn't have thought the man would whisk them all away in the middle of the night, with little afterthought about how it would affect Kyle. And what about Morgan? Did it take her weeks, months…maybe a year to get over the loss? Did she think about Kyle when she was giving birth to their daughter? What about the five years that followed? His heart thumped wildly, realizing he hadn't asked a really important question.

"Is Morgan married?"

Landon shook his head. "No. She's not married."

"Boyfriend?"

Landon grinned. "No."

"I'm glad you're enjoying this. My life has been tossed upside down, and who knows where I'll end up." He thought about Lexie. His first priority would be to make contact with her somehow.

Landon stilled his expression. "Look, I know you have a lot of questions. Neal, Morgan's father, will be the one to fill you in on anything we haven't covered."

"Yeah, I know who Neal is. I've known Morgan and her parents since I was a kid."

"They're all good people." Landon glanced at Sean, who was snoring lightly, his hands still poised above the laptop keys. Then he turned back to Kyle. "Morgan is super nervous about seeing you," he said in a whisper. "If you've got any sort of anger toward her, you need to stow it before you see her. She's dealing with a tremendous amount of stress, and adding you to the mix just complicates everything even more."

Kyle wanted to bark back at him that someone needed to recognize the amount of stress he was under, but despite everything, he'd loved Morgan with all of his heart at one time, and he didn't want to cause her extra pain. He assumed that having a sick child was overwhelming. But the only thing overwhelming Kyle was fear—of losing Lexie over this.

But as much as he loved Lexie, he couldn't push a Pause button to mute thoughts about Morgan and

Emma. He wondered if he was even father material. He had no feelings for this child one way or the other, except that he could save a life, something he'd do for anyone if he were able. Emma might be his daughter, but the lack of knowledge about her made it hard for him to accept the emotional impact that he might have expected.

"I'm going to do my best not to upset her, but no promises." Kyle looked at Sean when the man shifted his weight in the seat, but once he was snoring again, he said, "If you don't want me to upset her, then maybe you need to let me tell Lexie what's really going on so I'll be a little calmer." He shrugged, raising an eyebrow. "I'm going to tell her when I get back anyway."

"You mean, if we don't kill you, right?" Landon grinned.

A shot of adrenaline backstroked through his veins until he was sure it would come out his mouth in the form of vomit.

"Kyle... everything is going to be okay. Really." Landon still spoke in a whisper. "No one is going to kill you. You have an opportunity to save your daughter's life. And you can tell Lexie all about it when you get home."

Kyle scratched his forehead. "How can that be? I haven't had contact with these people for almost six years, but it will be okay for me to tell Lexie all about them?"

"Just wait for Neal to talk to you."

"Well, I hope he clues me in better than you are." Kyle huffed, leaned his head back, and attempted to pray. But his thoughts were so jumbled, he wasn't sure God could even sort them in a way that made sense.

"Oh, there's one more thing." Landon scowled. "And we should have mentioned it earlier. Morgan is Mia. Her mother, Patricia, goes by Patty now. Neal is Alex. You'll need to get used to those names. And their last name is Smith."

Kyle stared at Landon for a few long moments. "*Mia?* Morgan doesn't look like a Mia."

"Well, that's her name now. We agreed to refer to them all by their previous names until you settled into things. But now would be a good time to associate their faces with their new names."

Kyle tried to attach the name Mia to the Morgan he'd loved. It didn't fit her. "Did she choose Mia or one of you guys?" He nodded toward Sean.

"It was selected for her."

"Wow." Kyle rolled his eyes. "Will someone be *selecting* a name for me too?"

Landon grinned. "Uh, no. You get to stay the same ol' Kyle you've always been."

I don't feel like the same ol' Kyle.

Lexie stared at the email on her phone as she trembled from head to toe. Then she re-read it for the tenth time.

Lexie,

I know this will come as a surprise, but I feel like I need some time to myself to think about things. I'm sure I'm just having a touch of cold feet, so please don't worry. We have the rest of our lives to spend together, but there are a few things that I need to take care of before we are married. Can I please ask you to just trust me about this? Our love can withstand this. Trust me, okay?

I love you,

Kyle

She'd been sitting on the couch for the past hour and jumped when there was a knock on the door. "It's open." She'd called her mother as soon as she'd received the email.

"I could barely understand you on the phone. Are you okay?" Her mother sat down beside her. Lexie showed her the email on her cell phone and waited for her to read it.

"I don't understand." Her mother handed the phone back to her, pressing her lips together for a few moments. "What does this mean?"

Lexie swiped at her swollen eyes and shrugged. "I have no idea. And I've emailed him back, sent a text message, and tried calling, but there's no answer."

"Honey, you have to have a clue. You're planning to marry this man in a few months. Did you two have a fight or something?"

Lexie wondered if she should have called Penny or one of her other friends, someone instinctively more sympathetic than her mother. "No. We didn't have a fight, and nothing has changed."

Her mother huffed, then said, "Well, you were concerned earlier today because you hadn't heard from him, not even a text. Did you have some sort of gut feeling that something was wrong?"

"Mom!" She said it louder than she meant to, enough that her mother leaned a few inches away and scowled. "Nothing was wrong. There've been plenty of times that one of us hasn't been able to text for a lot of reasons. But this…" She took her phone back from her mother and skimmed the email again. "This is bizarre." Sniffling, she tossed the phone on the couch next to her.

"Okay, okay." Mom stood up and began to pace. "Have you been to his apartment?"

"Kind of."

"What do you mean, *kind of*? It's just a few steps away. Don't you think you should go see what's up?"

Lexie stood up, straightened her crumpled pink shirt, then blew her nose. "I'm not going to snoop. And if he wanted to get away from me, he wouldn't be in his apartment right downstairs." She folded her arms across her chest and looked down. "Besides, I already went to his apartment and beat on the door, but I was too nervous to use my key."

"Chop, chop." Her mother clapped her hands twice. "Get the key."

Lexie was too desperate not to reconsider the idea, so she shuffled toward her purse on the kitchen bar. She held the key in her hand for a few moments before she said, "Okay. I'll go look. Just to make sure nothing seems off."

Her mother hurried toward the door. "I'm going with you."

A few minutes later, Lexie put the key in the lock, jiggled it, turned it back and forth, but the door didn't open. Her heart thumped against her chest as she turned to her mother, tears pouring down her face.

"The lock has been changed."

Chapter Four

Kyle stood up in the plane once it stopped. A couple more inches, and he wouldn't clear the ceiling of the jet, which Landon called a Super Midsize earlier. Both Landon and Sean had to bend over a little not to bump their heads.

He waited for the pilot to lower the steps, then Kyle followed his escorts down and glanced around. He'd never been in a private jet, so he wasn't sure of protocol, but they were a long way from the LAX main terminal. He'd noticed earlier that the pilot had taxied away from the tarmac. His mind was a thunderstorm of activity. *I need to find a way to call Lexie. I have a daughter. I'm with the CIA in a private jet. And I'm going to see Morgan after all these years.* Maybe his priorities were out of whack, but getting in touch with Lexie was at the top of his list.

"I need to go to the restroom." Kyle nodded toward the terminal as he stuffed his hands in the pockets of his jeans.

"There's a bathroom on the plane," Landon said before making his way to the pilot.

Oh yeah. They'd told him that when he boarded, but Kyle didn't leave his seat the entire flight. He turned to Sean. "Where am I staying? When will I see Morgan—I mean *Mia*?" He swallowed hard. "And the little girl."

"Soon." Sean was reading something on his cell phone and frowning.

"Okay. So, where am I staying?" He grunted. "It better be the Penthouse or Presidential suite somewhere, after all of this."

Sean stowed his phone, barely smiled, and said, "I'm sure you'll be pleased with your accommodation once we arrive at our final destination."

Kyle tried to read Sean's expression, but it was flat, and as Kyle looked around, he saw two guys refueling the plane. "Do what?" His head pounded like it might explode. He wasn't sure he could process any more information today.

Sean took a step closer to him. "Kyle, this airport isn't where Morgan and Emma are. We are just refueling."

The hairs on the back of his neck prickled. "Okay, you know what… " Kyle puffed his chest out, knowing he was no match for Sean, but wanting some answers. "You told me we were going to California!"

Sean's eyebrows bent inward as he scowled. "Lower your voice. Everything is fine."

Kyle ran through a string of curse words in his mind, but he stowed them and took a deep breath. "With all due respect, Sean…everything is not *fine*. My life just got overhauled, and now I don't even know where we're going. That's a bunch of—"

"Honolulu. That's where we are going." One side of Sean's mouth curled up. "Surely there are worse places to be going."

"I can think of worse places to be taken during a kidnapping." Kyle rolled his eyes, and under different circumstances, he'd be thrilled to be going to Hawaii.

"We told you, Kyle, no one is kidnapping you."

"Then why didn't you just tell me we were headed to Hawaii, instead of letting me believe California was our destination?"

"We wanted to be sure the situation was secure first."

Landon strolled back up to them as Kyle looked back and forth between the two men, wondering which one of them packed the most powerful punch. Just in case Kyle lost control and took a swing at one of them.

"Well, I didn't even bring swim trunks," Kyle said as he forced a fake grin.

"I doubt there will be time for swimming or walks on the beach." Landon took in a deep breath and blew it out slowly, looking at the pavement. When he looked back up at Kyle, he said, "I just pray you're a match for Emma. The doctors will do some tests, but as her parent with the same blood type, everyone is hopeful."

Kyle stared at the man. There was enough emotion in Landon's comment to know that he cared about the little girl. "Have you known Emma all of her life?"

Landon smiled as he glanced at Sean. The older man's flat expression lifted at the sound of Emma's name also. "We both have," Landon said. "She's a beautiful little person."

Kyle was quiet. He didn't know this girl. And it didn't sound like he was going to have an opportunity to get to know her. He'd do the right thing, then go back home to Lexie. But as soon as he faced the possibility that he might not see the child again, it pierced his heart. "Do either one of you have children?"

Landon shook his head, but Sean nodded. "I have two daughters and three grandchildren."

Kyle thought for a few moments. "Then, can you, for one moment, understand some of what I'm feeling? I just learned I have a daughter." He didn't think he was having the right feelings, though. Shouldn't he feel more than he was? Was he missing the paternal gene? Either way, he hoped at least one of these fellows would warm up to him a little.

"I do sympathize with your situation, Kyle." Sean nodded toward the pilot, and it looked like the refueling process was complete.

Kyle got in step with both men as they walked back to the stairs leading into the plane. "But wait... " He stopped in his tracks, forcing Sean and Landon to wait for him to finish. "After this trip, then I just leave, go back to Houston, and I never see Emma again?" Staying in his daughter's life seemed like the respectable thing to do, if it was possible. "Or, now that I'm in her life, will I be able to stay in her life? See her grow into an adult, get married?"

Landon's gaze seemed to be somewhere outside of their circle, but Sean locked eyes with Kyle. "If you are a match for Emma, the doctors will schedule the stem cell transfer. From there, you will recover, then return home. You won't see Emma again."

Kyle took a step backward, fists clenched at his side. He had no idea how he would feel about this child, but this entire charade was unfair—and just plain wrong. "How can you just calmly say that?" He was almost yelling, and maybe the events of the day had caught up with him, but he could feel tears in his eyes. "Dude, I'm on emotional overload right now. Seriously. My fiancée is at home reading some stupid email that she'll never believe." He pointed a finger at Sean. "I'd like to know exactly what that message said, by the way!" He took a breath as he put a hand to his forehead, hoping to calm the thunder. "And then I just go back home and resume my life as if none of this happened?"

Sean and Landon exchanged glances while Kyle waited for one of them to tell him to lower his voice or smack him. Landon cleared his throat.

"Yes, that's right. You'll go home with the knowledge that you have a child, but you won't ever see her again."

Are you stupid? "I'll know they are in Honolulu, and I'm sure I can find them again."

Landon folded his arms across his chest, glanced at Sean, then back at Kyle. "Morgan and Emma don't live in Honolulu. It's simply where the best hospital is located, and that's where the procedure will take place."

Kyle hung his head, shaking it.

"But…" Landon said. "We're not as cold and heartless as you think."

"I doubt that," Kyle mumbled without looking up.

"You'll have options." Sean nodded to the pilot, signifying they were ready.

"What options?"

"You can choose to stay." Sean started toward the stairs again, Landon following.

Kyle hurriedly got in step behind them. "What do you mean, *stay*? Like, Lexie and I would live in the same state as them? Or just write letters and have Emma every other weekend and holidays? What options?"

Sean lowered his head and walked into the plane. Landon turned around from where he was standing on the top step. "No, Kyle. That's not how it works. You can choose to stay with Morgan and Emma, but you could never go back to your old life. You wouldn't see your mother or Lexie again. That's the way this arrangement works. It's not really a witness protection program, but similar."

Kyle lowered his head, almost tripping on the steps. "This is crazy," he said, fighting tears. But he stayed quiet. If the little girl triggered feelings in him that he couldn't fight off, he'd figure out a way to stay in her life. Somehow. And one thing he knew for sure. He was never giving up Lexie.

Tourists paraded past Morgan in waves bigger than the morning surf. Some wore fresh leis while others still sported the cheesy fake variety. Suitcases and carry-on bags adorned with "Aloha!" stickers and "Hang Ten!" tags trailed behind hurried airport pedestrians.

Morgan brought a hand to her chest when Sean and Landon came into view on the escalator descending to baggage claim, where Morgan was standing. Seconds later, her eyes locked with Kyle's, and for a few moments, she was seventeen again, cocooned in a blanket of youthful love and absorbed by everything that went along with it. She hadn't expected this. Maybe she'd been so absorbed with Emma that she hadn't allowed herself to feel what it would be like to see Kyle after all these years. He was taller, she thought. His brown hair was shorter, and his blue eyes seemed a shade darker. But as she studied him walking toward her, she willed away any feelings lingering in her heart. He'd be gone soon enough. And this time there would be goodbyes. She glanced at Landon and Sean, but quickly refocused on Kyle. He stopped right in front of her.

"Morgan," he whispered.

"It's Mia now." She held her breath, tempted to throw her arms around him and hold on for the rest of her life. "Thank you for coming," she managed to say, her voice cracking.

"We have a daughter." Kyle said matter-of-factly, as if the realization hadn't soaked in yet.

"Emma," she said. Since her daughter was born in Hawaii, she'd always be Emma Smith. No need to change her name like the rest of them did, giving up a past without leaving a trace of the life they'd lived.

Kyle's glassy eyes couldn't mask his emotions, and Morgan wished she could tap into his mind and read his thoughts. Was there still love? Resentment? Anger?

Landon cleared his throat. "We need to get going."

Morgan didn't move or allow her eyes to drift from Kyle's, afraid that if she blinked, that he'd be gone again. He inched forward until he was close enough that Morgan could feel his breath against her skin. Cupping his hand behind her head, he drew her to him, and she clutched his shirt with both hands, squeezing her eyes closed.

"We have a daughter," he said again in a whisper.

"Yes." Morgan buried her head in his chest. "Emma."

Landon cleared his throat again, louder this time, and Morgan forced some distance between her and Kyle, then she glanced at Landon, knowing all of this was hard on him also.

Chapter Five

Lexie, a box of Kleenex, and her wedding dress sat atop her bed, and every time she thought she couldn't cry another tear, a bucketful streamed down her face. She jumped when her cell phone rang and quickly slid her finger across the Answer button on her phone. "Hello."

She waited, but there was only static. "Hello," she said louder. "Kyle?" The number wasn't his, but she stayed hopeful.

More static, then the line went dead, her small window of hope closing. She held the phone in her hand, but after thirty minutes, she finally tossed it on the bed. Everything about this situation was wrong. She'd already been to the apartment manager's office the day before, but the woman wouldn't share any information about Kyle's lock being changed, saying she couldn't discuss it with someone not on his lease. Lexie doubted that was true. It had been obvious several times in the past that the woman had a thing for Kyle. Lexie wasn't the jealous type, so it hadn't bothered her. Until now. Everything was up for grabs. *Does Kyle have someone else?* She didn't think so. *Why did his feet become suddenly cold? What does he have to take care of?*

"Please, Kyle. Call me. Please be okay," she murmured to herself.

She picked up the phone and looked at the number, then Googled 808, the area code. *Hawaii?*

It must have been a telemarketer, maybe someone trying to sell her a vacation, but she hit redial anyway, and all she heard was static.

She lay down, pulled her wedding dress toward her, and latched onto it. Then she prayed that wherever Kyle was, that he was safe.

Kyle looked out the hotel window, and if not for the mountains in the distance, he would have thought he was in Houston or any other metro city. *Couldn't they have at least sprung for a room with a view of the beach?* Sean had said this hotel was near the hospital where Emma's procedure would take place, assuming Kyle was a match.

He stared at the phone, but all his attempts to reach Lexie had resulted in one possible connection, and there'd been too much static to know if she was on the other end of the line. Anger burrowed into Kyle's heart like a tick sucking the life out of him. He was a prisoner of his own circumstances, and even though he knew Morgan—Mia—was a victim in her father's charade, he was mad at her too. She'd offered up very little information on the ride to the hotel the night before. *I deserve better than this.*

It was a selfish thought considering the situation, but as each second clicked by, his anger rose, and by the time someone knocked on the door, he was shaking with rage. He was going to tell Sean and Landon a thing or two. He yanked the door open, and his jaw dropped.

Neal was almost completely gray, and the lines of time had found their way to the corners of his eyes. "Hello, Kyle."

Taking a step backward, Kyle inched to one side so Neal could come into the room, then Kyle closed the door. He was torn between hugging the man or punching him, so he did nothing but force his jaw back into position.

"I want to see Emma." He wanted to see Morgan, too, but he didn't want Neal to read anything into that. Surely Morgan hadn't changed so much that she hadn't felt his pain the night before.

"I know this all must be such a shock to you." Neal shook his head, frowning. "I wish that things had gone differently, but the situation is what it is." He smiled, but barely. "You look good, Kyle."

"I have to reach my fiancée." He pointed to the phone. "And I know your guys disabled the phone somehow, but Lexie is in a panic, I'm sure."

Neal scratched his forehead, and for a moment, Kyle thought he was considering the idea, but then he remembered how Neal always scratched his forehead when he was thinking. "The situation isn't ideal," he said, still rubbing two fingers parallel with the lines above his eyebrows. "We will move things along as quickly as possible so we can get you back home."

Kyle's hands balled into fists at his sides. "This is all a bunch of—"

"Then why did you come?" Neal's voice rose a fraction as he posed the question.

Kyle grunted, then shrugged. "I'm not going to let a child die if I am able to save her, especially since she's my..." He swallowed back a lump in his throat."...my daughter." The word still sounded strange, but maybe if he said it over and over again, the action would generate more of an emotional attachment. "When am I going to meet Emma?"

"Soon. But first we need to find out if your bone marrow is a match. If not, we can put you on a plane back home right away. There won't be a need for you to meet Emma." Neal walked to the window, pushed the curtains open more until sunlight filled the room. But even the bright island sun couldn't lift the tension from the room.

"Are you out of your mind?" Kyle walked toward Neal, but stopped when Morgan's father turned around scowling. "I just found out that I have a daughter. Do you think I'd really leave here without seeing her?"

Neal sighed. "I suppose that could be arranged."

Kyle rolled his eyes. "I would hope so." He took a step closer to Neal, realizing he didn't know this man anymore. Did he ever know him? "You were like a father to me," he said in a shaky voice.

Neal lowered his head for a few moments before he looked back at Kyle. "I can still be like a father to you while you're here."

"That isn't how parenthood works. Or so I'm told. You all stepped out of my life with no warning. Just gone!" The memories pierced his heart as he recalled walking around the Calhoun's empty house, but he forced himself to gain control and stay focused. "Does Emma know that I'm her father? Is she old enough to understand all of this?"

Neal sat down in one of two chairs on either side of a small table in the corner. A fresh orchid contrasted the sterility in the room. "She understands that she's sick, but it doesn't seem fair to tell her that you are her father, only to have you disappear from her life again."

Kyle clenched his fists at his side. "It's not like I'm being given a lot of choices."

"Life isn't fair."

Kyle slouched into the other chair. "A bit cliché, don't you think?" Arguing with Neal wasn't going to help. Kyle assumed Neal was running the show. "So, what is the plan?"

"We've pulled some strings to move this process along faster than normal, and we have a team of doctors in place. First stop is the hospital." Neal scratched his head again, frowning. "Morgan insisted that the two of you have lunch together once you get your bone marrow drawn, so I've arranged that after the hospital visit." He paused and lowered his hand. "I'll be honest, Kyle. I don't think it's a good idea for you and Morgan to spend unnecessary time together. It will make it that much harder to say goodbye. But, as you know, Morgan is strong willed, and she wasn't going to take no for an answer."

"I have no idea if she is still strong willed." Kyle gazed across the room at a picture on the wall, a woman wearing a lei and advertising a cruise to Maui. But recreation was the furthest thing from his mind. He turned to face Neal. "Why hasn't Morgan married? It seems like she'd want a father for Emma."

Neal scratched his forehead again, and Kyle was thinking it had turned into more of a tic, as opposed to part of his thinking process. "Morgan stays closed off emotionally. She blames me for putting her in this situation."

"You can't fault her for that."

Neal frowned. "The situation isn't ideal, but keeping my family safe is always my first priority."

Maybe you shouldn't have had a child. He squashed the thought right away. *Then there'd be no Morgan. Or Emma.* "Has Morgan been serious with anyone?" It seemed unlikely to Kyle that she wouldn't have dated and gotten close to someone.

"These are questions for Morgan." Neal stood up. "I think it best that we start referring to Morgan as Mia, even in private."

Kyle nodded, although she'd always be Morgan to him.

"Let's get phase one of this operation underway." Neal straightened his back, and slowly Kyle stood up too.

"Yep. Let's get going."

Kyle needed to call Lexie. *I'll borrow a cell phone from someone.*

Morgan sat on the deck at a table for two overlooking the beach, trying to tame her hair and wishing she hadn't forgotten a hairband. A salty scent pervaded the air as foamy waves crested and broke not far from where she sat, a flock of seagulls making their presence known. She turned and caught a glimpse of her father in the distance, and a second later she saw Kyle moving in her direction, his sunglasses making it hard to read his expression. Her father walked back to his car, but Morgan was sure Landon wasn't far away.

"Everything go okay at the hospital?"

Kyle pushed the glasses up on his head and nodded to a bandage on his arm. "Yeah, I think so. And they gave me a physical. At first I thought maybe my heart medication might be a problem, but they said it wasn't."

He gazed down at her, glanced at the ocean, and finally sat down. They hadn't said a lot in the car the night before. Maybe it was because they were tired. Perhaps because they didn't know each other anymore. Their lives had gone on. Kyle's had, anyway.

"What happens if I'm not a match?" Kyle must have been balancing that thought on the tip of his tongue, Morgan thought, as the answer punched her in the gut. Again.

"We'll keep looking."

Kyle hung his head for a few moments, and when he looked up at her, he had tears in his eyes. "This is all so messed up, Morgan."

"Mia," she said in a whisper.

He gazed into her eyes, and she'd have done anything to read his thoughts. But Kyle couldn't have changed that much. She was pretty sure she knew what was on his mind.

"You're worried about Lexie, right?" Morgan reached for her glass, wishing it was something stronger than water. She wasn't a drinker, but her nerves were frayed beyond what she could have imagined.

Kyle nodded. "Yeah. I am. We're engaged, and there is no way she's going to buy that cheesy email that Landon and Sean cooked up."

Morgan smiled a little, her heart pattering in her chest as she remembered a time when Kyle felt that way about her. "Wow. You really love her."

He hung his head, then gazed out at the water. Morgan did, too, lost in memories. Hues of aqua and emerald tumbled together as the tide rolled up on pristine sand with a splash. The natural landscape was breathtaking, but today Mother Nature was only a temporary distraction.

"It's okay, Kyle. I prayed that you'd find someone, that you'd be happy. I really did."

He locked eyes with her. "I prayed about you too." His expression was flat. "Mostly that you'd contact me."

"The whole thing wasn't fair. I wouldn't speak to my father for weeks. My mother would barely talk to him either. Your mom was her best friend, and she really missed her."

"My mom missed her too."

They sat quietly for a while, the wind tossing Morgan's hair across her face, the familiar smell of saltwater swirling in the air.

"Do you think we're being punished?" A pained expression fell over Kyle's face. "I mean, for what we did. We always said we would...you know..." He raised one shoulder and slowly lowered it. "We said we would wait, until we were married."

Morgan smiled. "I used to wonder about that too." She paused as she recalled holding Emma for the first time. "Until I held Emma. I looked at her, and until that moment I had no idea that a love that strong existed. I felt closer to God at that moment than ever before in my life. I remember thinking how God loved His own son this much—or more—and sacrificed Him for all of us." She took a deep breath. "So, I can't believe that anything to do with Emma was a mistake. It was part of God's plan. But..." She wasn't sure how much to share with Kyle, but since she hadn't aired her feelings aloud, she decided to go for it. "But I don't understand God's plan. I lost you, then I was gifted with this beautiful girl, and now..." Her eyes filled with tears. "I might lose her," she said in a shaky whisper.

Kyle reached across the table and held her hand, a gesture that felt as familiar as the smell of the ocean. "We won't lose her."

Morgan noticed he used 'we', and there should have been some sort of peace in knowing that everything was coming out in the open. But as she gazed past Kyle, Morgan saw Landon far enough away that he wasn't noticeably visible, almost completely hidden behind two large plants near the entrance—yet close enough that he could be at Morgan's side within seconds. She eased her hand away from Kyle.

"Is there someone in your life Morgan?" Kyle peered across the table as he rubbed his chin.

She blinked back her earlier tears to make room for more as she looked at Landon again.

"There used to be," she said.

Chapter Six

Lexie sat next to Kyle's mother. Across a desk full of files and stacks of paperwork, a Houston police officer looked at them like they were nuts. Lexie's mother had wanted to come, too, but she had a longstanding doctor's appointment and opted to catch up with Lexie and Diana later. Lexie thought that was probably just as well. Her mother would have pounced on this cop and probably made things worse.

"I'm telling you, something isn't right. Kyle would never change the lock at his apartment without telling me, and there is no way he wrote this email." Lexie glanced at Kyle's mother and she nodded.

The cop—his badge read *Officer Scott Siewert*—leaned back in his chair, shaking his head. "Ma'am, the guy said he needs time. I'm sure he'll surface soon. We can't file a Missing Persons Report based on the information you've given me."

"He didn't write that email." She pointed to the printed copy of Kyle's email she'd placed in front of the man.

There was almost a hint of a smile. "So, someone hacked his email, changed his lock, and kidnapped him?"

"We're upset," Diana said. "We don't need sarcasm. If Lexie said Kyle didn't send that email then I believe her."

Officer Siewert stood up, and Lexie suddenly felt very small. The guy was huge, tall like a towering live oak, and as he leaned forward a little, Lexie knew their time was up. "Call me in a few days if you're still worried."

Lexie and Kyle's mother slowly stood up. Lexie supposed she'd think the same thing as the police officer if she were on the other side of the desk. But she knew, beyond a shadow of a doubt, that Kyle didn't write the email or request that his lock be changed. She'd have to keep praying he'd call her. And she'd have to keep asking God to keep Kyle safe, wherever he is.

Morgan offered a vague run-down for the past five and half years of her life, avoiding locales, and even names of people she'd known, including whomever it was that she'd been involved with for more than a year. It broke Kyle's heart to see that all the animation Morgan once had was gone, the way she used to talk with her hands, laugh out loud, and sometimes even snort when she was really tickled about something. *Robotic.* That was the word that came to mind now. He wondered how much of the change was due to her father's situation. or maybe most of it was because she had a very sick child. *Our child.*

"How'd you meet Lexie?" Morgan fidgeted with her napkin on top of the table. They'd both ordered the special—Kalua Pig. Kyle still didn't have much of an appetite, even though the offering looked a lot like pulled pork, a favorite of his.

"College," he said as he shifted his weight in the chair.

Morgan stared at him before she raised an eyebrow. "Which college?"

Kyle recalled all the dreams he'd shared with Morgan at one time, including both of them wanting to attend the same college. Kyle had held onto that. "Sam Houston State." He swallowed hard as he waited for a reaction from her, but she just bit her lip and nodded. "I'm a teacher, history."

Morgan nodded again, but didn't say anything. She'd already told him that she hadn't attended college, that at the time she was angry with her father—and pregnant. The only way she knew to rebel against her father was to refuse to further her education. Then Emma was diagnosed when she was three.

Kyle glanced around the outdoor seating area of the restaurant. "I need a restroom."

Morgan pointed over his shoulder. "I saw a sign when we came in."

He forced a smile, then headed that way. Inside the safety of this private area, he loitered around, waiting—for someone with a cell phone. There was a guy in one of the stalls, but an older man came in, and Kyle approached him.

"I'm here from Houston, and I don't have my cell phone." He nodded to the man's IPhone strapped to his belt. "I've got a bit of an emergency. Do you think maybe I could borrow your phone? I promise, two minutes tops. I need to call my girlfriend."

"Sure." The man unhooked the case and handed the phone to Kyle. He typed in Lexie's number as fast as he could, but hit End when the door to one of the stalls creaked open and closed.

Kyle lowered his gaze and handed the stranger his phone. "Thanks, but never mind." He stuffed his hands in the pockets of his jeans and turned to Landon, who was glaring at him.

After the older guy left, Landon said, "Maybe once you meet Emma, you won't feel the need to put everyone's life in danger."

Kyle could feel the burn in his cheeks. "I don't want to put anyone's life in danger. I want to let Lexie know that I'm okay, and I'm going to keep trying until I succeed."

Landon took a step closer, a muscle tensing in his jaw, along with a large enough stride to send Kyle a step backward. "It's my job to protect this family, specifically Mia and Emma."

"Can't I just call her and tell her I'm okay? I don't even have to tell her where I'm at."

Landon's expression was one of pained tolerance as he squinted his blue eyes. "You just told a complete stranger that you're from Houston."

Kyle sighed, feeling stupid. "Whatever." He turned and left the restroom, deciding to think on this, not wanting to put anyone in harm's way, but talking to Lexie was a need, not a want. He slid into his chair, slouching into the cushioned back, and eyed his Kalua Pig. Morgan hadn't touched hers yet.

"I ran into our chaperon in the bathroom," Kyle said as he picked up his fork. "Or babysitter. Whatever you want to call him." He opened his mouth to take a bite but felt the daggers Morgan was throwing his way, her brown eyes narrowing into tiny slits. "What?" He put the fork down and gazed across the table.

"That *babysitter* has kept me and Emma safe for five years. He's also been a huge comfort to me during all of this. He'd protect me and Emma with his life, and not because it's his job, but because he cares about us." She gazed out at the crashing waves as she fingered a locket around her neck.

Kyle wondered whose picture she wore around her neck. *Probably Emma's.* He lowered his head, shook it, then looked back up. "I'm sorry. I'm glad that he looks after you and Emma. I'm just worried about Lexie, and it irritates me that I can't make one simple phone call to her." He rubbed his chin, his mind swirling about ways to make that happen. Landon couldn't be with him every second of every day. He didn't think.

"I'll talk to Landon and see if there's any way someone can get word to her, without sacrificing Emma's safety."

Kyle stared at her, still waiting for some profound feeling to overtake him and catapult him into the world of fatherhood, a place where he'd put his life on the line for Emma. *Isn't that what I'm doing, though?*

He leaned his head back until he was staring into a cloudless, blue sky. Sighing, he readjusted his gaze to Morgan, really took in her features. He should have been thrilled that she was going to go to bat for him about Lexie. But right then, at that moment, the way the wind tossed her blonde hair, the way she was looking at him, memories flooded his mind. "We had so many dreams," he said in a whisper, a voice that seemed to trail into the air and out to the ocean.

She smiled. "Yes, we did."

They were quiet for a while. Kyle finally took a bite of his pork. It tasted a little like pulled pork back home, but with a smokier flavor. Morgan wrapped a small amount around her fork and finally took a bite also.

"Pretty bracelet," Kyle said, not usually one for small talk, but it was a cool bracelet. He could feel them both taking silent trips backward, and it wasn't going to do any good to rehash the what-ifs.

Morgan glanced at her wrist. "Thanks."

Kyle took a closer look. "Are those all shells?" They were beautiful, but he'd never seen anything quite like them. Bright pink shells no bigger than the eraser on a pencil were interspersed with pink and white striped shells about the same size.

Morgan held her wrist up, twisting it so he could see it from all angles. "Yeah, all shells. My mom made it from shells she's collected where we live." Her eyes rounded for a few seconds as she pressed her lips together. Then she blinked and cleared her throat.

Kyle wondered if she was going to admit her mistake, that she'd given him a clue. He eyed the bracelet again. There were only two types of shells on Morgan's wrist. They had to all come from the same place.

"It's okay," he said. "You didn't spill the beans, so don't add that to your list of things to worry about."

She gathered her hair at the nape of her neck and slung it over her shoulders, but several strands took flight and swept across her face anyway. "It's hard to keep anything from you."

Well, you've done a pretty good job of it. Kyle finished chewing and swallowed. "Did your dad *do* something? I mean, what could possibly lead to all this secrecy?"

"I don't know." There was no hesitation in her response. Kyle believed her right away. She set her fork down on her plate when her phone rang in her purse.

Kyle finally took another large bite as Morgan rummaged for her phone. Once she'd answered, the call lasted less than a minute.

"You're a match," she said after she hit End. Then she covered her eyes with one hand as she stretched her other hand out to Kyle. He grabbed her hand and held it tightly as her lip trembled. When she uncovered her eyes, she dabbed at the tears pooling in the corners, letting go of his hand. "You're going to be the one to save our daughter."

Maybe it was the way she said it, or the fact that she was crying. Maybe it was relief mixed with fear, spurning some unidentifiable emotion that was foreign to Kyle. He didn't think he told his legs to move, but the next thing he knew, he'd rounded the table, she'd stood up, and Kyle pulled her into his arms. "Yes, I'm going to save our daughter."

For the first time since he'd learned he had a child, Kyle allowed himself to feel the meaning in that statement. And for the first time since he'd arrived, he decided he was going to make Emma the priority. Everything would be back to normal when he went home. Lexie would understand, and Emma would be well. But as Kyle held Morgan in this surreal world he'd entered, he was sure nothing would be normal again.

Lexie stood beside the guy she'd hired to break into Kyle's apartment, knowing the snippy apartment manager wouldn't waste any time having them both thrown in jail if they were caught. Lexie had taken a chance and asked the young groundskeeper if he wanted to make some quick cash.

"Can you go any faster?" she said in a whisper in the partially lit hallway outside the apartment. She hadn't told her mother or Kyle's mother that she was going to become a criminal if that's what it took to find out what happed to Kyle. Diana had said earlier that she was researching private investigators, but Kyle's mother didn't have the kind of money to actually hire one, nor did Lexie. If things became more desperate, Lexie might ask her parents for help.

She was a little surprised that her mother hadn't offered to do more, but Lexie's parents weren't fond of giving up money.

"You're in." The young guy pushed the door open, then ran his hand through long strands of dark hair.

Lexie handed him a hundred dollars, cringing that she was encouraging this teenager to break the law. But he'd barely taken the money when Lexie scooted past him and into Kyle's apartment. She closed the door quietly behind her, then hit the lights, expecting to see toppled furniture, a smashed lamp, maybe the bookcase overturned. But as she scanned the living room, nothing looked out of order, and even the remote control for the television was in its designated spot on the coffee table. *Kyle, where are you?*

She scurried from room to room with no idea what she was looking for. After about ten minutes of aimless searching, she flung herself onto the couch. Guilt nipped at her.Even though this was to be her home in a few months, it seemed like a huge invasion, barging into Kyle's apartment this way. She leaned her head back against the couch and prayed.

I need help, God. What should I do? Is Kyle in danger? Am I misreading everything? Does he really want time away from me or have cold feet? Please, Lord, give me the eyes to see things clearly, the ears to hear Your wisdom, and the courage to remain strong and faithful amidst any challenges I might face.

After a while, she shuffled around Kyle's apartment, got a drink of water, and decided this was a waste of time. She'd sunk to a new low, but surely Kyle would understand. Once she found him. Her stomach rolled and tumbled as she walked toward the front door, an uneasy swirling that terrified her. *If anything happened to Kyle…*

She pulled the front door open, but turned for one last look around. Something shiny underneath the coffee table caught her eye, a shiny silver object about the size of a dime. Closing the door, she made her way to the table, reached down and picked up a cufflink. Turning it over and over in her hand, she didn't think Kyle owned any cufflinks, and it seemed odd for one to be in the living room. There was something written on the back, but it was way too small for her to see.

Lexie fumbled around in her purse until she found her cell phone. She set the cufflink on the coffee table and took a picture. Her hand trembled as she enlarged the photo on her phone. And as she read the inscription, her pulse picked up. Kyle had never been to Niihau Island, that Lexie knew of. She Googled the island and found out where it was. Alarms sounded loudly in her head. It was an island in Hawaii. And Lexie had gotten a phone call from a Hawaii area code. *Coincidence?* She didn't think so.

Chapter Seven

Kyle's feet were rooted to the tile floor outside of Emma's hospital room. She—his daughter—was only there for more testing, now that they'd learned Kyle was a match. Morgan had met him in the parking lot, and Landon agreed to give them some time alone together while he parked.

"She's just here for the day, but there's a lot of waiting around and they had a vacant room." Morgan shrugged. "It's more comfortable in here." She reached for the door handle, and Kyle grabbed her arm.

"Wait." His heart thumped wildly in his chest. "I know she doesn't know who I am. But does she know…?" Sweat pooled across his forehead as the relevance of the next few minutes slammed into him like a Mac truck.

"She knows you're the man who will make her feel better." Morgan eased out of his grip, then put her hand on his arm. "Kyle, it will be fine. And remember to call me Mia, even in front of Emma—especially in front of Emma. She's never known me as anyone else."

Kyle took a deep breath and followed Morgan into the room, his eyes instantly locking with the little girl sitting on the bed. She was wearing a pair of white shorts with a pink blouse. Her feet hung over the side of the bed, her toes curled into a pair of pink flip-flops. Golden ringlets of hair were pulled into short pigtails on either side of a pale face offset by bright blue eyes. Morgan had already told him Emma had endured a round of chemo in preparation for a transplant, and that Emma's hair was still growing in, thinner than before. Ultimately, the transplant hadn't occurred due to medical reasons Kyle didn't completely understand. He hoped there wouldn't be a problem this time. It just seemed wrong that any child should have to go through chemotherapy.

She was a cute kid, and Kyle didn't think he felt that way just because she shared his genes. But there was no doubt that Emma was sick. Morgan had explained the symptoms of asplastic anemia. Emma had bruises on her tiny pallid arms and legs, very little color in her face, and she was frail.

"Emma, this is the man we've told you about, Mr. Brossmann." Morgan went to her daughter and placed the back of her hand against Emma's forehead, but only for a couple of seconds.

Kyle forced his eyes away from Emma's and looked at Morgan. "Does she have to call me Mr. Brossmann? Maybe just Kyle?" Dad wasn't an option, and Kyle felt relieved about that at the moment. Anything else added to his overloaded heart and mind could cause him to unravel completely.

"Sure." Morgan smiled, then folded her hands in front of her. Kyle held her gaze for a surreal few moments.

"Mr. Kyle, thank you for coming a long way from your home to help me to get well." Emma barely smiled, but when she did, Kyle's insides swirled and flipped. Her tiny voice was as dainty as she was. He had a strong urge to hug her, but he had no idea what was appropriate.

"You're welcome." He forced a smile as he glanced at Morgan. "Um, how do you feel?" Kyle faced off with twenty-five seventh graders for a good part of the year, and he'd been told he was good with children. But he'd never felt so out of sorts as he did right now.

"I'm hungry."

Morgan let out a small gasp as she lifted up on her toes. "That's great, Sweetie. What do you want? I'll get you whatever you want."

Kyle took a deep breath and made his way to a chair. He'd never been so wobbly on his feet, until the past couple of days. He remembered his father watching reruns of a TV show called The Twilight Zone when he was a kid. Weird shows with people in unusual situations. Kyle felt like a participant in his own episode. *Morgan is a mom.* He'd barely had the thought when his stomach flipped again. *And I am a dad.*

"Chocolate ice cream," Emma said. And when her face lit up in a smile, Kyle was glad he was sitting down. An odd feeling settled over him in a way that seemed like it should feel good. Something warm cocooned around his heart, holding it, yet melting it at the same time. Before he liquidized into a puddle on the floor, he forced a burst of adrenaline to cool his heart. *Self preservation.* He didn't want to get close to Emma.

But as Kyle stared at this child of his, he wasn't sure that would be an option.

Morgan knew better than to leave Emma alone with Kyle. They'd all told Emma how important it was not to tell anyone where they lived, especially the man who was coming to help her. But that was a lot of pressure for a little girl, even one who is healthy and well. And Morgan had already slipped up at lunch, so she knew how easy it was to do.

They all turned when the door to Emma's room opened, followed by heavy footsteps. Emma jumped from the bed and ran to Landon. It was the fastest Morgan had seen her move in the past couple of weeks.

"Landon!" Her voice had a signature squeak normally, but even more so when she was around her 'bodyguard' as she called him.

"Hey, Emmie Lou." Landon scooped Emma into his arms and kissed her on the cheek. Morgan turned to Kyle.

"Her middle name is Louise, and Landon has called her Emmie Lou since she was born." Her eyes drifted back to Landon, then over to Kyle, then back to Landon, as her past collided with what had nearly been her future. Emma loved Landon, as much as Morgan did, maybe more. The breakup had been hard on everyone. But as she refocused on Kyle, there was still pain where he was concerned, even all these years later. She'd vowed to never get that close to anyone again. But having him here was stirring feelings she hadn't expected. What-ifs were all over the place. Her father would give Kyle an opportunity to stay, to be a father to Emma. Morgan wondered if he would even consider the offer. It was a horrible position to be put in; leave your fiancée forever or never see your daughter again. And what about Morgan and Kyle? Was there a chance they'd fall in love again? Could she open her heart again to her first true love? She slowly looked at Landon, and as their eyes locked, she could see the same questions in his gaze.

"Let's go get our girl some ice cream," Landon said, and Morgan instinctively started to go with them, but stopped.

"Um. Are you going to be okay for a few minutes? If a nurse comes in, can you let her know we went to get ice cream?"

Kyle nodded.

"Do you want some?"

"Nah. Ya'll go ahead."

Kyle didn't move for a full minute after the trio left. He stared at the phone, and he'd never wanted or needed Lexie more than right now, but he couldn't help but wonder if this was some sort of test. Landon had made sure he was in the bathroom earlier when Kyle tried to borrow a phone. And now, they just leave him alone with a phone three feet away?

He stood up and paced, then finally picked up the phone and listened to the dial tone. *It works.* Slowly he pressed Off and set the phone back on the table next to the bed, then walked to the window. As he gazed past the buildings that partly obstructed his view of the ocean, he thought about how he'd always wanted to visit Hawaii. *Here I am, and I just want to go home.*

He leaned his head back, stared up at the ceiling, and blew out a long breath before he refocused on the phone again. The temptation to call Lexie was almost too much to resist, but he couldn't bear the thought of putting Emma, Morgan, or any of them in danger.

It hadn't taken much for Kyle to figure out that Landon was the person Morgan had been involved with. In the few minutes Landon had been in the room with them, he noticed the looks going back and forth between them. It angered him that Landon had hurt Morgan, but there was also some sort of twisted relief that Morgan hadn't given her heart completely to someone else, which made no sense since Kyle was madly in love with Lexie.

Morgan sat down in the waiting room next to Landon, who was finishing his second ice cream cone, while Emma made her way to the toys in the far corner.

"I don't think you should be testing Kyle this way." She spoke in a whisper so Emma wouldn't hear, thankful they were the only ones in the room. "I'm sure he's calling his girlfriend. And if he's not calling from the phone in Emma's room, there are plenty of other phones in the hospital."

"We just want to know if he's going to put Emma's safety and needs first." Landon's gaze bordered on a glare before he shoved the last of the cone in his mouth.

"It doesn't really matter if he does or doesn't. Either way, he's agreed to this procedure. Then he'll go back home to Lexie, and that's that." She shrugged as she tried to keep her expression level and void of all the emotion she'd bottled up over the past two days.

"Will he? Go home?" Landon paused, his eyes now fixed on Emma. "Or will Emma steal his heart too?" He turned to Morgan, the muscles in his neck tensing at the base of his square jaw. "Or maybe the two of you can make a go of it."

Morgan wanted to tell Landon that she was having those same thoughts, but why twist the knife in Landon's open wound any more than she had? "That's not going to happen."

Landon turned to her as the professional mask he usually wore slowly retracted, revealing the tenderness of the man she loved. "I want you to be happy, Mia. I love you and Emma, you know that. But I'll step aside and request a transfer somewhere else, if you can have a life with Kyle, the three of you as a family."

"No." Just the thought of Landon leaving set her insides on fire. "No," she repeated, shaking her head. She'd broken up with Landon three months ago, following two years of an infatuation between them that escalated into something much more. At first, she'd thought her feelings for Landon came about because of the way he loved Emma, the way he protected both of them. But then she'd realized she was in love with the man, not the bodyguard or CIA agent. Just Landon. It was then that she began to pull away. Her heart wasn't up for grabs again. But Kyle being here was stirring up emotions she hadn't expected. She wasn't sure if it was the bond of having a child together, the fact that he was marrying someone else, or pure jealousy that his life had gone on just fine without her, and she couldn't commit to the man she loved.

Until now, she hadn't made time to psychoanalyze her situation. Did she avoid committing to Landon out of fear of losing him? Were there unresolved feelings about Kyle? Lost in thought, she jumped when Kyle entered the waiting room. He slowed his steps as he walked by Emma, who barely noticed him.

"A nurse came by while ya'll were gone." Kyle's eyes shot to Emma again before he took a few more steps toward Morgan and Landon. "But it was actually me she came to see. I'm going to have to get some shots that will build up my stems cells prior to the transplant."

Kyle sat down on the other side of Morgan and propped his elbows on his knees before he lowered his forehead to his hands. He had to be exhausted, physically and mentally. Morgan wished she could hold his hand. She wished she could hold Landon's hand too. Both were men she loved in confused capacities, remnants of her past fused with the present, leaving her uncertain about her future.

Morgan glanced at Emma before she looked back at Kyle. He took a pill bottle from his pocket and popped the blue and white pill in his mouth. Another reminder of their past and the many messages she'd left for him. She smiled a little. He still didn't need any water to wash it down.

"I didn't call Lexie," Kyle said without lifting his head. "Just in case that was some sort of test or something."

Morgan glared at Landon, but he wouldn't look at her. He was watching Emma quietly building a tower of blocks that looked like it might topple over any second. She elbowed him until he turned her way, then mouthed. "Help him."

Landon sighed. Then shook his head.

Morgan loved this man, but she wondered if she'd ever get past the power of the position he held, where sometimes things just weren't negotiable. She reached into her purse, pulled out her cell phone, then elbowed Kyle this time.

He straightened in the chair as she pushed the phone toward him.

"Call Lexie."

"What?" Kyle scowled as his eyes shifted to Landon. He didn't reach for the phone, and Landon also had a sour look on his face.

Morgan stood up, tossed her phone in the seat so hard that it fell and hit the carpeted floor. "I need peace. I need Kyle to stay focused, and he deserves a chance to get to know Emma." She lowered her voice to barely above a whisper. "And not while he's stressing about his own situation at home and missing his fiancée."

"Fix this, Landon. Do something."

She hurried to Emma about the same time all the blocks fell over, scooped her into her arms, and left the two men in the waiting room, both with dropped jaws.

Chapter Eight

Landon stood up right away and took two or three steps toward the door, but then stopped and turned around. Kyle eyed the phone on the floor, unsure whether to pick it up.

"Don't call your fiancée from that phone." Sighing, Landon scratched his forehead. "I'll talk to Sean and see about getting you a secure line."

Kyle stood up and walked toward him. "I see on the news all the time that terrorists communicate in code, so I don't understand why I can't call Lexie."

"You don't understand a lot of things." Landon stood taller, if that was possible, then headed toward the door.

"Hey." Kyle caught up to Landon just as he reached for the door handle. "I could do without the attitude." He took a deep breath and released it slowly. "Is contacting Lexie really going to put Emma and Morgan in danger?"

Landon scowled. "Mia. Her name is Mia. And you can probably make a phone call to Lexie on a secure line. But the call isn't the issue. Lexie is the issue. Every contact with the outside world puts Mia and her family in danger. I don't know how much Alex told you, but I can tell you this... Alex was undercover for a long time, and some really bad people found out, the type of people who aren't going to give up looking for him. Ever."

It took Kyle a few seconds to make the connection that Alex was Neal, Morgan's father. "Lexie would never do anything to put anyone in danger. And I trust her completely. I know everything about her. She's going to be my wife."

One corner of Landon's mouth curled up. "I doubt you know everything about her."

Kyle grit his teeth as the veins in his neck tensed. "There is nothing worse than a person in a position of power who uses it to torment others. I know everything I need to know about Lexie."

Landon's expression went flat, void of emotion, something he was able to do within a half second. "Is that what you think I'm doing, tormenting you?" He stepped closer to Kyle, his chest puffed out as his face turned red. "I don't care what you think. The only reason you're here is for Emma." He paused. "Right?"

Now it was Kyle whose mouth took on a saucy grin. "You're afraid I'll choose to stay, and even though you broke up with Morgan, you don't want me in her life. You don't want her, but you don't want anyone else to have her."

Landon held out his arm like he was going to grab Kyle around the neck, but he pulled back and held both arms rigid at his sides. "I didn't break up with *Mia*. She broke up with me. I love her, and I love Emma like she's my daughter."

Kyle held his position, but when Landon blinked his eyes a few times, Kyle thought he might actually cry. The big, tough CIA man was getting watery. "Then why does Mor—*Mia* get so upset when she talks about how she was involved with someone? It was pretty easy to see that it was you by just watching the way you two look at each other." He shrugged. "I just assumed you were the one who broke up with her."

"Well, you assumed wrong." Landon gained his composure quickly. "Mia's closed off her heart. She says she's afraid of getting hurt. But I'm wondering if that's the gist of it, or if it has something to do with you."

Landon's comment made Kyle's heart sing a little, then Lexie's gorgeous face flashed in his mind's eyes and a wave of guilt washed over him.

"I'm not staying. I'm going back to Lexie. I'm sure that *Mia* is afraid of getting hurt again, but I'm not the one who hurt her. It's not like I broke up with her and fled. If someone is at fault, it's her father."

Landon let out a long burst of air he'd seemed to be holding. "I'll go find you a secure line."

Kyle put a hand on the door, closing it before Landon could pull it all the way open. "No. I'm not going to call Lexie." He heard the words slip from his mouth, and he wanted to take them back, but a driving force wouldn't allow it. "I'm not going to be the one to put Emma, or any of them, in danger." Something niggled him. "Is there something I need to know about Lexie?"

Landon rubbed his chin as he shifted his weight and avoided Kyle's eyes. "No," he said before he forced the door open and left.

Kyle didn't move, unsure whether or not to believe the guy.

Lexie sat on her parents' couch, all of them quiet. Even her outspoken mother seemed at a loss for words. Finally, her father spoke up.

"Sweetheart, it could all be coincidental. The phone call from Hawaii and the cufflink with Niihau Island engraved on it. If Kyle hasn't been to Hawaii, then the cufflinks could be a gift from someone. And the phone call could have been a telemarketer. You know we all love Kyle, and his leaving is a reckless thing to do, but I think you have to accept the fact that the boy's got cold feet and he's off somewhere sorting things out in his mind."

Lexie didn't even realize she was shaking her head, until it started to pound again, the way it had for the past week. She'd called the unhelpful police officer again, but he remained—unhelpful. "I know Kyle, and I trust our love. He doesn't have cold feet."

Lexie's mother tucked her feet underneath her on the other end of the couch and cleared her throat. "Honey, I'm going to have to agree with your father. What does Kyle's mother think? I'm sure she's worried sick, but what are her thoughts about all of this?"

"Of course, she's worried." Lexie tried to keep the snappiness from her voice, but when her father grimaced, she knew she hadn't been successful. "She has a wealthy cousin that she hasn't spoken to in years, but when she contacted him, he offered to chip in for a private investigator to look for Kyle." *Hint, hint.* "Apparently he isn't as wealthy as Diana thought, or he's fallen on hard times. Either way, she's still short on the retainer to hire help."

"Did you know that Niihau Island is referred to as the forbidden island? There's not even two hundred people living there, and it's mostly closed off to anyone except for residents' relatives and invited guests." He paused. "I Googled it."

Nice way to change the subject, Dad. "I know. I looked it up on the Internet too."

They all grew quiet again. Lexie heard the Cuckoo clock in her old bedroom crow six times. Her stomach rumbled and growled, but she hadn't been able to eat much.

"Maybe this is for the best," her mother said, followed by a heavy sigh.

Lexie put a hand on her chest as she fought to swallow back tears. "How can you say that?"

Her mother twisted on the couch to face Lexie. "Honey, we love Kyle. You know that. Originally, I thought you two needed to wait a while longer to get married, but I can see how much you love each other. But Lexie, you've never been completely honest with that boy."

Lexie's heart missed a beat. Then another beat. Then it felt like it stopped and she was dying. "How can you even bring that up right now?"

"Starting a marriage while keeping a secret that big just isn't healthy." Her father forced the footrest of his recliner to the floor, then sat taller and leaned forward. "You need to tell him, Lexie. He's going to find out."

"I know," she said in barely a whisper. "And if I can find him, I will." She should have done so a long time ago, but there'd never seemed to be a good time. Fear had wrapped around her like a boa squeezing the life out of her every time she'd tried to tell Kyle her one secret, the only thing she'd ever kept from him. But right now, she just prayed he was safe.

Morgan's mother hugged Kyle so tight that he couldn't breathe.

"It is so good to see you." Patricia—*Patty*—cupped his cheeks in her hands, smiling. He'd always called her Mrs. Calhoun anyway. *Smith,* he reminded himself. "You're as handsome as ever," she said. Patty backed away and sat down in a chair across from Kyle's hospital bed, where he'd spent the past four days. "I'm so sorry that you've been alone these past few days. Emma has been sick to her stomach. She gets really down and out sometimes because her immune system is weak. It was taking both Mia and me both to take care of her." She grimaced a little. "This wasn't the best time for *Alex*..." She waited, as if to make sure Kyle knew Alex was Neal."... and Sean to get called out of town, but they'll be back before the transplant. How are you feeling? I understand they kept you in the hospital because you were having some side effects from the medication they're giving you."

He nodded. "Yeah. Mostly headaches and nausea. But I don't really think I need to be in the hospital. Is Emma okay now?" He was worried about the girl. Maybe his paternal gene was kicking in after all.

"She's doing much better." Patty smiled as her eyes filled with tears. "Kyle, the circumstances surrounding the way we left so quickly must have been devastating for you. It was for all of us, also, and I know you were left with a lot questions." She blinked her eyes, forcing the tears back. "How is your mom doing? Alex has kept an eye on all of you, so I know she never remarried. But is she okay?"

Kyle wasn't sure whether to be grateful or creeped out. "Yeah, she's okay. She missed you for a long time."

Patty lowered her gaze. "I still miss her," she said softly before she looked back up at Kyle. "And I know there is a part of Mia that will always love you. You must be so confused and upset about all of this."

"It's not ideal," he said as his stomach roiled and churned. "I think I'm going to be sick." He hurried out of bed and toward the bathroom, hoping his hospital gown was covering his backside. But flashing Patty was the least of his worries as his stomach rejected the lunch he'd eaten earlier. He threw up. Over and over again.

"Can I get you anything, Kyle?" Patty talked to him through the closed bathroom door.

"No." He hurled again and reminded himself that he had a daughter who was very sick. This was nothing compared to that. Another round of heaving, and he finally washed his face and exited the bathroom. Patty was standing by the bed with a hand over her mouth.

"They said this might happen," she said. "Some people have some fairly strong side effects from the medications they use to pump up your stem cells."

Kyle shuffled in his socked feet back to the bed and sat down. "It's okay." He allowed himself a long look at Patty. She looked exactly the same, as if Kyle had been at their house the day before, back in Houston. "I guess Mor…uh, Mia…is at home taking care of Emma?"

"Yes. She wanted to come instead of me, but when Emma feels that bad, she wants her mommy." Patty smiled. "And I wanted to see you anyway." Pausing, she smiled a little. "I hear you're getting married."

Kyle nodded. "Yeah, her name is Lexie." He was sure Patty already knew that. "We're planning to get married in the fall."

Patty nodded, but Kyle could see the sadness in her eyes.

"I guess I'd always thought you'd end up being my mother-in-law some day."

"Me too," she said barely above a whisper without looking at him.

They were quiet for a while. Finally Kyle asked, "Why do you think Mia broke up with Landon?"

Patty stiffened from the chair she'd sat down in. "Mia told you about Landon?"

"No. Not really. She told me she'd had someone in her life, but not anymore. Landon sort of spilled the beans about that, but I was already onto both of them. "It's the way they look at each other." Lexie flashed into his mind again.

Patty smiled. "Landon is a wonderful man. But I think that there is a fine line between protection and control, and sometimes Mia doesn't want to be controlled."

Despite everything, Kyle chuckled. "That doesn't surprise me."

"But..." Patty locked eyes with Kyle. "I'm not sure she ever got over losing you. I know she's closed her heart somewhat, or that's what she says, that she doesn't want to get close to anyone after what happened with you. But Landon would never be yanked out of her life. If anything, in that regard, he is the perfect person for her. That's why I think that you still hold her heart, or at least a part of it, and maybe she isn't being completely truthful with herself."

Kyle didn't know how to respond. His emotions were all over the place. "Maybe because we were each other's first love." He knew he still had feelings for Morgan, and he always would. But when he tried to envision a life without Lexie, he just couldn't do it.

"Maybe," Patty said, then a nurse walked in.

"How's our boy?" Nurse Karen was about Patty's age, and Kyle already knew that she had four boys; six, nine, twelve, and fourteen. She'd been the only person Kyle had really talked to. Landon had been in and out, and Kyle knew he was hovering around all the time. Except today. He hadn't seen him in a while. But otherwise, it was just the two nurses rotating shifts. Francine, the other nurse, wasn't particularly friendly.

"I've been throwing up a lot." Kyle opened his mouth when the thermometer grew near. He'd learned the drill. Next was blood pressure.

"I'll be here in Honolulu for a while, so I'll come check on you later." Patty stood up, then kissed him on the forehead before she left.

Again, Kyle felt like he'd just been at Patty's house, eating dinner with the family, Morgan and him holding hands under the table. *So familiar.* He closed his eyes and pictured a life with Morgan, pushing Lexie as far from his mind as she was geographically. But while he waited to see whose image would rise to the forefront, the face that strolled into his mind easily was Emma's.

Chapter Nine

Two days later and with full island sun, Morgan walked along the beach with Kyle. His body had finally recharged itself after the side effects of the meds. She wanted to hold his hand, if for no other reason than to signify their combined efforts to get Emma well.

Glancing over her shoulder, she spotted Landon and Emma downwind of them. Emma busied herself pointing at shells and critters at the edge of the water, and it warmed Morgan's heart to see her daughter feeling so much better. Emma and her bodyguard were far enough away to give Morgan and Kyle some privacy, but close enough that Landon would see Morgan holding Kyle's hands, if they did. She'd never do anything to hurt Landon, but her memories continued to collide with what the future might hold. They were quiet as they met almost head on with a group of tourists, maneuvering closer to the water so they didn't run into them. Morgan regretted that Kyle wouldn't be seeing more of the islands while he was here. *Or will he?*

"I'm sorry you were left by yourself for a few days." She pulled a strand of hair from across her face, reached for a twisty on her arm, then wrangled the whole mess into a ponytail.

"Uh, you wouldn't have wanted to be around me anyway. I was busy throwing up a lot." Kyle turned to her. "But your mom stayed with me most of the day, so." He paused, shrugging. "It was nice to be mothered since my own mom can't be here. And it reminded me of that time I fell off of my skateboard right in front of your house when we were kids. Your mom is the one who doctored me up."

"I remember that day." Morgan gazed out over the ocean as the waves lapped at her bare feet. "I remember lots of things."

"Are we going to play the 'what if' game?"

Morgan forced a smile. Two large parts of her heart were trailing behind her, but a third was walking beside her. "I guess we could, but everything that's happened up to now has led us to this moment. I'm so angry with God and so grateful to Him too." She glanced over her shoulder. "This will be the last walk on the beach Emma will have for a long time. She'll be in the hospital for at least a month after the transplant."

Kyle looked over his shoulder for a long while. "If all goes as planned, she'll go on to live a full life, a healthy life?"

"If all goes as planned," Morgan said, smiling, as she studied Kyle's expression. "She's beautiful, isn't she?"

He nodded, then finally faced forward again. "I know you can't tell me, but you must be staying close by. Can I at least ask if this is your first time to Hawaii too?"

Morgan swallowed hard and chose her words carefully. "We've been here for a while anticipating your arrival." She'd basically avoided the question. She tried not to lie when she was questioned, but instead to offer a variation of the truth. "But I've seen some of the other islands since we've been here. You'd like Maui and the other islands better than this one." She nodded to the tall buildings to their right. "But we needed to be at the best facility for the transplant, and that's here in Honolulu."

They walked quietly for a while. She'd always thought she knew Kyle so well, but time had a way of altering everything, and right now, she had no idea what he was thinking about. Lexie, most likely. Morgan wanted to feel sympathy for the woman Kyle was going to marry. But a tinge of jealousy nipped at her also.

"So…" Kyle stopped, leaned over, and rolled his jeans up a little. When he stood up, he locked eyes with her. "When this is all over, I just get on a plane to go home. I won't ever see you or Emma again. And I'm supposed to do this because it's the right thing to do. I'll tuck my feelings away…" He took a deep breath."…and walk away from you and Emma. Again."

Morgan's heart fluttered as she tried to read into his statement. Was he going to miss them both? With little regard for anyone else, she blurted out the first thing that came to mind. "Then just stay."

They stood facing each other, the ocean swirling around their ankles, and the briny smell of the ocean wafting up their nostrils. And it took everything in Morgan's power not to kiss Kyle in the most inappropriate way. He was in love with someone else, and Landon wasn't far away—but at the moment, the only thing that kept her from doing so was her daughter. She looked over her shoulder at Emma skipping along beside Landon. Her daughter wouldn't understand. And Landon surely wouldn't either.

"I'm considering it."

Morgan's mouth fell open. "You're considering staying?" Surely, she'd misunderstood.

Kyle's eyes cut past her to Landon and Emma before he refocused on Morgan." Why can't Lexie and I live wherever you live—or wherever you and

Landon live—however that plays out, then we can all be a part of raising Emma?"

Morgan's heart dropped to the pit of her stomach. She'd been foolish to think that maybe Kyle wanted to be a family, the three of them. Without Landon and Lexie. But even as she had the thought, she couldn't imagine her life without Landon.

"I don't think that's how it works." Morgan started walking again, and Kyle got in step with her.

"Emma is my child too."

Here we go. Her mother had warned her this might happen, that Kyle could pull the legal card. She'd fiercely defended him and said he wouldn't. "So, are you going to fight me for custody now?" *You can try.* She looked back at Landon, knowing that wasn't even a remote possibility. But her blood ran cold just hearing the possessive implication in Kyle's voice.

"I would never do that." He stopped and faced her again. "Emma doesn't even know me. I've spent barely more than a few minutes here and there with her since I've been here. My entire world is upside down. I want to know my daughter. I want to know her, Morgan!" Kyle lowered his gaze, and Morgan touched his arm, but he flinched and jerked away from her, then looked her in the eyes again. "I want to know her, Morgan."

She decided not to correct him on the name issue as tears pooled in the corners of his eyes.

"I'm going to give my daughter my stem cells, and I'm blessed and honored to be able to do that." He blinked his eyes a few times. "Then your bodyguard over there..." He nodded toward Landon and Emma."...will send me packing. And you'll fly back to wherever it is you came from."

Well, not exactly. Niihau was a short flight or boat ride from Honolulu. Morgan couldn't find any words of comfort.

"Will I get a graduation picture? A wedding picture? Will I know that she's okay and well?" Kyle blinked his eyes a few times and warded off any tears, but Morgan could tell he was struggling not to break down. "And don't tell me that life isn't fair. I get that. Totally. I lost my dad. I lost you. And now I'm going to lose Emma too."

Morgan reached for him again, but he took a step backward. "No. Just don't."

"Kyle, what can I do?" She eased forward, and he didn't back up this time." Tell me. What can I do to make this easier for you?"

He raised both his shoulders, then dropped them slowly as he blew out a long gust of air. "I have no idea. I'm no match for your dad or your CIA boyfriend."

"He's not my boyfriend." Morgan looked at Landon and Emma growing closer. Landon was carrying Emma now, which meant her daughter was already getting tired.

"Well, he used to be, and maybe he should be now. Emma needs a father, and if I can't be it, then maybe it should be Landon. She obviously loves him." He shook his head. "I don't even know how to feel. I want to have a bond with Emma, and I want to love her—just not too much. That probably sounds awful, but a guy can only take so much heartache. And I might have another big one coming when I get home and face Lexie. She has nothing to do with any of this, but I can't even imagine how much she's suffering."

Morgan forcibly pulled Kyle into her arms and held him. He cupped his hand behind her head and eased her cheek onto his chest. "Tell me what to do, Kyle."

He eased away. "I don't know." Kyle dabbed at his eyes before any tears spilled, and he smiled as Landon and Emma got closer. Landon set Emma down in front of Kyle.

"Mr. Kyle, are you crying?" Emma pushed her white sunglasses up on her head and walked closer to him. Kyle squatted down in the sand and faced her as she cupped his cheeks in her small hands. Morgan held her breath. Even at five, Emma had always been sensitive and compassionate. Something she'd gotten from Kyle.

"Not really crying, but I think I need a hug," Kyle said barely above a whisper.

Emma released her hold on his cheeks and threw her tiny arms around Kyle. "Mommy says when times get tough, we put our worries into a big giant bubble and blow them to God. He catches the bubbles in heaven and takes care of everything." She stepped out of the hug and scrunched her face into a serious expression, her lips pressed together in a thin smile. "Do you want us to make a bubble for your troubles?"

Poor Kyle. He was having trouble maintaining much composure, but Morgan could see him still trying to keep any tears in check.

"I think that's a great idea." Kyle stood up, smiled at Morgan, then he and Emma emulated a big circle and blew the invisible bubble filled with worries and prayers to heaven.

"Maybe you two want to take a walk together," Landon said, a slight smile on his face, as he glanced at Morgan.

That most likely meant that Landon wanted to talk to Morgan alone. When Emma reached for Kyle's hand and they started down the beach, Morgan brought a hand to her chest. Emma was smiling and chattering away. She prayed her daughter would remember the rules about what not to say.

After they were out of earshot, Landon said, "We need to talk."

"If you want to talk about me hugging Kyle, he was just upset. Nothing more to it."

Landon hung his head for a few moments, then looked back up at her and sighed." Mia, I'm not going to be that person. I love you and Emma enough to want you to be happy, whether I'm in the picture or not. I've told you that. If you choose to be with Kyle, I'm not going to fight it." He gently held both of her arms, the waves breaking closer to their feet and seemingly louder than before.

Morgan gazed into his eyes. She opened her mouth to speak, but nothing came out.

"I know you're confused. This is a bizarre situation, and I really and truly feel badly for Kyle. And I've heard repeatedly from you—and even your mother—that you're scared to let anyone get too close for fear of losing them again. I need to know if that's really what caused you to break up with me, or is the reason walking down the beach with Emma? I need to know that, and you need to be fair to yourself, me… and Kyle. Because, I'm here to tell you, if you'll let me into your heart again, I promise to never leave you, no matter what." He took a breath, looked out across the water, and looked back at Morgan. "I would always figure out a way for us to stay together. But I don't want to be a second choice if you're going to spend your life harboring feelings for another man."

Morgan looked down the beach at Kyle holding Emma's hand, her daughter slowly walking alongside him and smiling. Morgan looked on for a few seconds before she wrapped her arms around Landon's waist and buried her head in his chest.

"Mia, I love you and Emma with all my heart." He kissed her forehead.

"I know you do," she said softly in the comfort of his protective embrace. She snuck another look at father and daughter. The man she'd once loved, the daughter they'd created, and the possibilities that loomed before her now.

Life had never seemed more confusing.

Chapter Ten

Lexie sat on her couch staring at the television that wasn't even on. She kicked her feet up on the coffee table and slouched into the cushions. Life as she knew it had ended. It was a dramatic thought, but everything she'd believed in was in question. She prayed continuously to hear from Kyle, but she'd become so physically ill from worry that her parents had tried to talk her into moving back home, which wasn't an option for Lexie. That would mean she'd accepted that Kyle wasn't coming back, and she didn't believe that.

Kyle's mother called every day, and Lexie knew Diana was worried sick, but the woman had a job to go to every day, so that was a distraction. Lexie was off for the summer, but even if she hadn't been, not even teaching could have distracted her from the hundreds of scenarios she'd dreamed up about what could have happened to Kyle. She closed her eyes.

God, if Kyle isn't meant to be with me, I'll live with that. But I just pray with all my heart that he is okay. Please God, keep Your loving arms around him.

She reached into the bag of Cheetos next to her on the couch, forcing herself to eat a few, then she lay her head back against the couch, wishing sleep would come and knowing it wouldn't. Her lids were heavy but they snapped open when her phone rang. She hurried to her purse on the kitchen table, found her phone, and almost fell over when she saw the 808 area code.

"Kyle, is that you?" She held her breath and waited but the phone went dead. With shaky fingers and a trembling lip, she hit Redial. A man answered on the first ring.

"Sir, I believe you just called me. Are you with Kyle Brossmann by any chance?" *Maybe it's his kidnapper.* She held her breath. "Please don't hang up."

"Um, I'm sorry for the call. I must have hit this number stored in my phone by mistake."

"I—I'm looking for someone. I think he's... missing. And I received a call from a Hawaii area code over a week ago. This is the second call, but I guess it could be a coincidence." Lexie thought about the cufflink and decided to press on. "Can you tell me how you think you ended up with my phone number?"

"I'm sorry. I have no idea. Where are you calling from?"

Lexie shook all over as her heart thumped in her chest. He didn't sound like a kidnapper. "I'm in Texas."

"No, I'm sorry. I don't know anyone in Texas, but I wish you all the best finding your friend."

"Thank you."

"Uh, wait a minute."

Lexie brought a hand to her chest. "Did you think of something?"

"Yeah, I did. I was in the men's room, and a young man asked to borrow my phone, said he was from Houston and needed to call his girlfriend. I handed him the phone, but I don't think the call even went through when he handed it back. Another man came out of the bathroom, and honestly the guy who borrowed the phone seemed a little spooked. He handed me the phone back and said never mind."

Lexie sat in a kitchen chair and tried to steady her breathing. "Can you tell me where in Hawaii you are?"

"Honolulu. If your friend is missing, have you called the authorities?"

"Yes, but they didn't feel there was enough to warrant a Missing Persons Report." Although she hadn't checked back with the police in a few days.

"Can I ask you one other thing, please? Can you tell me how far Niihau Island is from Honolulu?"

"I'm surprised you'd even know about Niihau Island. Many of the locals don't even know about that place. It's referred to as the Forbidden Isle or the Forbidden Island. There aren't many people living there, and until recently, only friends and family of the residents were allowed to visit. I think there are a few tourist boats that might go there these days. There's not even any electricity there, just solar power and generators."

Sounds like the perfect place to hold someone hostage. Lexie's mind was racing. "Is it far from Honolulu?"

"Honestly, I've never been there. You can take a boat or a helicopter, but I'm not too sure how long it takes. They've got Navy personnel out there and some government offices I believe. Biggest thing Niihau is known for are the lei pupa, their shell leis. They go for thousands of dollars, I've heard."

"If I text you a picture of the man who asked to borrow your phone, do you think you'd recognize him?" Lexie still had her hand on her heart.

"Maybe. I've slept since then. But you're welcome to send it."

Lexie maneuvered to her Texts, found a picture of Kyle, and said, "Don't hang up. I'm sending it now."

"I'm not sure I know how to check a text message while I'm on the phone, so if I lose you, I'll call you back."

Lexie waited.

"I got it. And yep, that's the kid from the restroom."

Lexie burst into tears. "Thank you," she said barely above a whisper.

"You're welcome. Godspeed to you. I hope you find your friend."

Lexie wanted to cry for a long time. But there was no time for that.

Kyle slowed his stride when Emma did. "Are you tired? Do you want me to carry you?"

Emma frowned. "No."

"Oh, uh...I saw Landon carrying you, so I just thought maybe... "

"That's different. He's my bodyguard." She looked up at Kyle. "But I want him to be my daddy. I've never had one, but Landon says it's up to Mommy."

Kyle felt a blow to his gut, but even worse to his heart. "So you must think Landon is a really good guy?"

"Yes." She smiled as her pace picked up a little. "He's strong too."

They walked quietly, but it wasn't long before Emma slowed down again. Kyle glanced over his shoulder at Morgan and Landon—hugging. Swallowing hard, he stopped walking when Emma squatted down to pick up a shell. Once they were moving again, Kyle took a deep breath.

"Do you get to walk on the beach a lot where you live?" He held his breath. What kind of person tries to trick a five-year-old? *A desperate father*.

Emma didn't look up, but just shrugged as she pushed her little, white sunglasses up on her nose. Then she held up a small shell for Kyle to see.

"It's pretty." He leaned in to have a closer look at the white shell, then Emma closed her hand around it and picked up the pace. His mind was full of questions, five year's worth, but Kyle didn't know where to begin, and his stomach was doing flips again, so that left him fearful he might hurl right there on the beach.

Kyle slowed down. "Emma…"

She stopped and looked up at him through her sunglasses. He squatted down, gently eased off her shades, and gazed into her deep blue eyes. Kyle didn't want to love her, but the emotion must be factored into the parental gene, which had reared its head over the past week. And now, he couldn't imagine leaving her. He wanted to tell his mother about Emma, scream it from the rooftops, tell Lexie, and fight Landon and Morgan to see her. But as he stared into this precious child's eyes, he knew he wouldn't do any of that. He'd die to keep her safe.

He saw Landon and Morgan out of the corner of his eye, but he didn't care. Time was running out. After he gave Emma his stem cells, he'd get shipped home, even though Emma had a long road to recovery ahead. He couldn't pull his gaze away from his daughter. *How can I have you in my life?*

"Everything okay?" Morgan asked as she stood next to Landon.

Kyle considered his options. He could fight hard to win Morgan back so they could all be a family. *But Lexie.* He couldn't imagine his life without her. Could he sacrifice Lexie to be with Emma?

He pushed back thin strands of golden hair from Emma's face. "Do you know what a beautiful little girl you are?" Kyle struggled to keep his voice from cracking.

Emma nodded and smiled as she pointed to Landon. "That's what he says too."

Kyle didn't look at the man who would most likely continue raising Emma, or at the least, be a huge part of her life. "I know you understand why I'm here, right?"

Emma nodded again. "To give me some of your stem cells to make me better."

Kyle took in another deep breath. "That's right. And wherever you go, you'll always have a part of me with you. And wherever I am, I'll always be praying you're okay."

Emma's bottom lip turned under as she gazed into Kyle's eyes. "I should give you something too."

You already have. "I think a hug would do."

Emma wrapped her arms around Kyle's neck and squeezed. He pulled her closer, swallowed back tears, and couldn't bring himself to let go of her, even when she started to ease away. *I love you, Emma. Feel my love.*

He finally let her out of his bear hug and put her sunglasses back on her. She handed him the shell. "Here," she said softly in her delicate voice. "You can have this."

Kyle held out his palm, and Emma dropped the small shell in his hand. Then she turned to Morgan, smiled, and walked to Landon. "I'm tired," she said. "Can you carry me?"

Landon scooped her into his arms. "Yep. Why don't we go find something to drink, and we'll let your mom and Mr. Kyle talk."

Emma waved to Kyle over Landon's shoulder. After they were out of earshot, Kyle sat down in the sand. More like folded into a lump in the sand. Morgan knelt down beside him.

"I can't believe you've done this to me." He heard how selfish it sounded the moment the words slipped from his lips. Clutching the small shell in one hand, he tapped his chest a few times. "I thought I'd die when you just vanished." Glancing down the beach at Landon and Emma again, his daughter waved. He raised his hand and tried to smile. "But now this. How am I going to say goodbye to her, Morgan? How? Tell me how, because I'm not sure I'll have the strength."

She lowered her head and put a hand on his leg. "Kyle, if you're wanting me to tell you I'm sorry for bringing you here, I can't do that." She looked up at him as tears started down her face. "You are saving our daughter's life. And I know it's at a great personal cost for you. I know this." She shrugged. "I don't know how to make things right. All I know is that because of you, our daughter should live a full life after the transplant. As long as there aren't any unexpected problems—and the doctors don't think there will be—then Emma will go on to lead a good life."

Kyle dabbed at his eyes, something he'd been doing a lot of. Part of him just wanted to let it all go and sob for hours. Another tear slid down Morgan's cheek.

"Do you have any idea how much I loved you?" Kyle held her gaze as he gently ran his thumb along her moist cheek.

She put her hand over his and pressed it closer to her cheek. "And I loved you." She lowered his hand, but squeezed it. "I still do."

Kyle still wasn't sure if he was going to throw up. He wasn't sure if it was from the medications he'd taken or the effort it was taking to suppress his emotions. He was sure he'd never watered up this much in his life. He pulled Morgan to him and held her while she cried as he struggled to keep his own tears at bay. When it seemed they had both exhausted all the emotion that had built up over the past five years, he looked at her, kissed her on the cheek, and leaned away.

"Do you love Landon?"

Morgan was sure that Kyle had been leading up to tell her that he was going to stay here, which would have complicated her life in several ways, no matter the emotional tug of war going on in her heart. "I love you both."

"We both love what we had." He nodded past her at Emma and Landon, who were almost out of sight, but Morgan knew Landon would never be completely out of sight. "And we love Emma," he said." "You know what I'm asking you. Do you love Landon, enough to make a life with him? I don't understand why you broke up with him. If he's not the one, then—"

"I thought you were the one." She glared at him. "And then I thought Landon was the one. But every time I allowed myself to be completely in love with him, I'd think of you, the way it all happened. I couldn't bear that again."

"Morgan." He shook his head. "Sorry, I'm never going to get used to you as Mia. Anyway, first of all, I don't know why you think that. He's CIA. He's probably the only guy in the world that won't get forced out of your life. If you love him, and he loves you, then maybe..." Kyle shrugged.

"What if he dies?" Morgan held her breath. The thought horrified her. "Every day for the past year, I've worried that Emma wouldn't get better. It's the kind of love that would make you easily die for another person. I started feeling that way about Landon. I loved him so much it hurt. I don't want to love that way. There's too much risk."

One side of Kyle's mouth curved up a little. "I felt that way about Lexie in the beginning, afraid I'd love her too much. Then lose her."

"I bet she's going crazy not knowing where you are. I wish things could have played out in a way that made things easier on you."

He was quiet for a while. Morgan was sure his emotions clawed and scratched at his heart the way hers were.

"How am I going to say goodbye to you and Emma again?" he asked again.

Morgan forced a smile. Even after all these years, she couldn't stand to see Kyle hurting this way. "With thoughts of getting home to Lexie."

"Lexie," he said in a whisper as his gaze drifted out to the ocean.

"Landon," she said softly, her stare parallel with his out to sea.

"Emma loves him," Kyle said a few moments later. "He would be a good father to her."

Morgan nodded. "He would." She reached for Kyle's hand, and for a long while, they both sat in the sand, watching the waves roll in, crashing not far from them, then the surf quieted, and the sea became calm.

Chapter Eleven

Kyle waited as a nurse took his blood pressure in the outpatient wing of the hospital. He was surprised that no one had come to be with him while he gave up his stem cells. Granted, it was an easy procedure, and he'd already been cleared to go home, but still. Maybe this was the beginning of the detachment phase. He'd already been told that his stem cells would be frozen until Emma was at her optimum health-wise.

"Pretty bracelet." He eyed the nurse's bracelet, almost exactly the same as the unusual one Morgan had worn the day at the restaurant.

"Thanks. I don't usually wear jewelry to work." She shrugged as she peeled off the blood pressure cuff from Kyle's arm. "But today is my birthday, so I made an exception. A bunch of us old ladies are going to kick up our heels after work." She chuckled. "Or try to."

Kyle smiled. "Happy birthday. I saw someone else wearing a bracelet like that. The shells are really pretty, different."

The woman held up her wrist. "This was a gift from my daughter and her husband. The shells come from Niihau Island and can't be found anywhere else in the world."

Kyle sat up on the bed and hung his legs over the side as his eyes opened wider. *Really?* "I've heard of Maui, Kauai, and some of the others, but not Niihau."

"The forbidden isle, we call it. Not everyone knows about it." She shook her head. "I couldn't live there. They don't even have electricity, just solar power. It's pretty detached from the rest of the islands."

Kyle wished he could get Lexie a bracelet like that, but he felt sure it was going to take more than a bracelet to get back into his fiancée's good graces. And he couldn't help but recall what Morgan said about her mother, that Patty had collected the shells where they lived.

"Have you seen Mia or any of the others this morning, the people that are usually here with Emma?"

"No, I haven't. But the weather is awful. It's been raining since I woke up this morning."

Kyle figured they didn't want to get Emma out in the rain, but Morgan could have come. Or Neal—*Alex*. Or Patty. Someone.

He tucked away any hurt feelings, and once he was cleared to leave, he hailed a cab to his hotel, wondering what the timeline was on his departure. He'd hoped that Emma would have the transplant before he left, but he could understand the doctors wanting her to be at her best.

But when he walked into his hotel room, he saw that the timeline for his departure had already been established. His small red suitcase was packed, and there was a letter on the bed.

Dear Kyle,

Saying goodbye again is too much to bear for all of us, and Emma wouldn't understand a tearful farewell. Please forgive me for this— and for everything we've all done to cause you pain. I hope you can feel joy and peace knowing you will be saving our daughter's life. The doctors have reiterated over and over again that fate had a hand in all of this. I know better, though. God has His hand on all of us, especially Emma.

"Joy and peace? Are you kidding me?" Kyle sat down on the bed and reminded himself to breathe.

A part of me will always love you. But Landon holds my heart, and I need to let go of my fears. You were right about Landon being a good father to Emma.

There is so much I could say right now, Kyle. But I know that there are no words to ease your pain. This is the life that God planned for us, and we have to make the best of it. I will think of you every time I gaze into our beautiful daughter's blue eyes.

I wish you all good things in life, and I pray that you and Lexie will live a wonderful life together filled with love and happiness. There is a commercial plane ticket home in your suitcase.

With love always,

Mia (and Landon, Dad, Mom, and Emma)

Kyle set the letter on the bed, folded his hands on his lap, and thought about his situation. He could sit here and cry or fight for his right to be with Emma. *I am not defeated. Yet.*

Lexie exited the boat at Niihau Island and wandered away from the other six passengers, despite the warnings that she could be in a heap of trouble with the locals if she was caught just wandering around on an island that didn't look kindly on outsiders. But as she rubbed the cufflink in her hand, she prayed that God would lead her to Kyle. The cufflink was the only clue she had.

She glanced down at her hand, void of her engagement ring. She'd pawned it to get a plane ticket, including a return flight. But she didn't know how she'd leave here without Kyle. After a full day of travel, she'd stayed in Kauai overnight, then booked a ticket on one of the few tours that came to Niihau. One maxed out credit card later, she fought the panic taking hold of her. She'd just spent a fortune based on a cufflink and a couple of phone calls. Not the Hawaii trip she would have imagined.

She waded in the bluest water she'd ever seen, getting further and further away from the boat she'd arrived on. The island had all the elements of a Hawaiian paradise at first glance, with the white sanded beach stretching as far as she could see. The biggest difference; it looked almost deserted if not for the boat with it's few passengers in the distance. The tour she'd paid for was for a half a day. There was no lodging, or even a restaurant on Niihau.

Despite her parents' pleading not to go, she'd made the trip anyway. After two flights and eight hours in the air to think, she'd come up with just about every scenario possible. Kyle had been kidnapped and was being held on this remote island. Why wasn't there a ransom call? Or Kyle had truly gotten cold feet and decided to get as far away from her as possible. *Nope*. She didn't believe that. Or another fear—that there was someone else, and they'd snuck off to get married and live in Hawaii. *Nope.* She didn't buy that either.

But a calling larger than her own thoughts and conscience had led her to Hawaii and onto the boat to this remote island. She eased away from the water and started her trek further down the unpopulated beach. After a while, she slung off her backpack and looked around. There was a village on the island. And she was going to find it.

Lexie bowed her head, put her palms together, and prayed.

Kyle sat down on his red suitcase near the water's edge. He'd tried to call Lexie a dozen times before he'd taken a boat to Niihau Island, but his phone still wasn't working. He'd tried from his hotel and a nearby restaurant on Kauai also, and no answer. Had she forgotten about him over the past couple of weeks? *No way.*

He was thankful the weather had cleared up and skeptical that Morgan, Emma and her family were here. But after he'd thought for a while, the only thing he had to go on was origin of Morgan's bracelet.

A little research later, and he confirmed what the nurse told him about Niihua Island. A long shot, but it sounded like a good place to shack up if you were in hiding. But he'd asked everyone he'd run into in the small village of Puuwai if they knew Mia, Alex, Patty, Emma, or Landon and Sean. Most just shook their head and kept going. One lady had told him to get off their island.

He only had a half a day to play detective. That was all the time an outsider was allowed on Niihau. And so far, the trip had been a bust. He sat on his suitcase, which he'd optimistically carted through the village hoping he'd find Morgan and Emma. Now he just felt silly. He stared out over the deep blue water, and attempted to pray.

God, I don't even know where to start...

He closed his eyes, but movement to his left snapped him to attention as a woman approached him. At that moment, he was sure they'd given him something at the hospital to make him go crazy. Maybe a drug to erase his memories or to make him hallucinate. It was a wild speculation from watching too many movies, but there was no way Lexie could be walking toward him.

As he stood up, his legs carried him toward someone, and when he got close enough to recognize his hallucination, he ran to her, threw his arms around her, and they fell to the sand in each other's arms.

And for the first time since all of this started, Kyle let go of the tears he'd fought to bottle up and sobbed.

Lexie kept her arms around Kyle as he cried, and it wasn't long before she cried along with him. Whatever had happened, he was racked with grief, and she couldn't stand seeing him in so much pain. But her own relief that she'd found him was enough to rattle her own resolve, and despite the torment, she could feel the love radiating between them.

When they both gained some composure, Kyle told her about his heartbreaking adventure, and Lexie cried the entire time.

"I thought for sure they were here. I felt called to come here, but now I know I was called here to run into you, not to find Emma." Kyle clutched both of Lexie's hands as he recounted the events. Even after they'd sat up, he'd never let go of her. "How'd you get here?

"I chartered a private boat." Lexie tried to control her trembling bottom lip. Now was surely the worse possible time to tell Kyle her secret, but she didn't know how much longer she could hold it in.

Kyle lifted her left hand and rubbed the top of her hand. "Lexie, where's your ring?"

"I pawned it before I left," she said through tears. "But I'll get it back."

"Oh, Lexie." Kyle lowered his head, shaking it. "No, I'll get it back. This is a trip you shouldn't have had to make." He gently cupped her cheek with his hand. "You're sunburned," he said.

Lexie wasn't sure how long they'd been sitting on the beach. Long enough that the tide had come up and they'd had to move back. "You are too."

Kyle stood up, pulling Lexie with him. "Let's find some shade and see if we can find something to drink."

They finally detached from each other. Lexie knew Kyle well, but she was wise enough to know that there was no way she could truly understand what he must be feeling. This was bound to play out emotionally, for both of them, for a long time. But for now, she praised God that Kyle was okay and that she'd found him.

An older woman with gray hair and a broom in her hand stepped outside a small house and walked toward them. "Do you have business here?" The dark skinned woman looked like she'd lived her entire life in the sun, with wrinkles that webbed across a thin face, spilled down her neck, and ran the length of her arms. Her dark hair hung long as she squinted her eyes and brought a hand to her forehead.

Lexie cleared her throat, knowing they both must look a mess with their swollen eyes and still covered in sand. "Um, we're looking for someone." She glanced at Kyle.

"The Smith family," he said. "Mia, Alex, Patty, and Emma." His voice cracked when he said his daughter's name. Lexie's heart broke for him, and she said another prayer.

The old woman pointed to her left. "Two blocks down, the big house with all the solar panels."

Kyle nodded, and he and Lexie headed in that direction.

"Wow. You must look more trusting than me," he said after they'd taken a few steps. "I couldn't get anyone to help me."

The closer they got, the faster Kyle walked. As the house came into view, Kyle let go of her hand, sprinted up the steps, and went straight to the window.

Lexie hurried to his side as the butterflies in her stomach fluttered and spun.

"Thank God," he said as he bent at the waist. "The last time this happened, I showed up at an empty house." Kyle knocked on the door. When no one answered, he knocked again. And again.

"They must not be home." Lexie's knees were weak. The entire trip had been surreal, but standing here on the porch with Kyle, knowing now that he has a daughter, and possibly about to be face to face with the woman he loved before her... she felt dizzy. She reached for Kyle's arm just as the door swung open.

A woman with salt and pepper hair and wearing an apron eyed them. "Can I help you?" It obviously wasn't anyone who knew Kyle, and the woman was holding a bottle of Windex.

"I'm looking for the family who lives here. The Smith family. Mia, Alex, Patty, and Emma."

"I'm sorry. They left the island this morning." The woman tipped her head to one side as she looked Kyle up and down before shifting her gaze to Lexie and doing the same thing.

"Do you know when they'll be back?" Kyle was trembling. Lexie reached her arm around his waist.

"They're not coming back. They moved. Left here for good. They'd rented the place furnished, and the landlord hired me to come clean and ready the place to lease again. This is the only house for rent on the island, so it will move quickly."

Kyle bent at the waist, and Lexie did her best to keep him on his feet. "I can't believe this is happening again."

Lexie kept her arm around him as his body shook with more tears. Lexie thanked the woman for her time as she led Kyle off the porch.

Chapter Twelve

Morgan buckled Emma into her seat by the window, as requested. Landon was on the other side of Morgan, and Morgan's parents and Sean were in the three seats in front of them. "I don't remember the last time I was on a commercial flight," Morgan said to Landon.

"It wasn't our first choice. Your father said our private jet was cleared to go, but there was a suspicious odor that the pilot couldn't identify, so your dad wanted to play it safe but still get off the island quickly." Landon spoke in a whisper.

Morgan reached for his hand, glancing at his wrist, and having a random thought. "I haven't seen you wear the cufflinks I gave you in a long time. You used to wear them even with your casual shirts."

Landon sighed, frowning. "I lost one. I was going to tell you, but I kept thinking it would show up."

"I would buy new ones for you, but they wouldn't be from Niihau Island. I'm guessing we won't see that place again." She paused, realizing she'd miss the quaint village with its friendly, if not a bit aloof, residents. "You're sure everything is okay with the transferring of Kyle's frozen stem cells?" She closed her eyes and leaned her head back for a few moments as the engine on the plane roared, preparing to take off.

"Yep. It's all being handled."

Morgan glanced at Emma, who was blissfully unaware of her circumstances. "The doctors said she is okay for now, but she'll need the stem cells soon." She sighed, then turned her head toward Landon and spoke softly. "I can't believe we did this to Kyle. Again."

"I know. I feel badly about it too. But there was just too much chatter again, and your father wouldn't have made this hasty move, especially with Emma sick, unless he felt strongly that you were all in danger."

"I'm so tired of living like this, Landon. Is this how it will be for Emma all of her life too?" Her mouth was almost in his ear as the plane started to taxi.

"No. I'm going to figure something out, so that both of you aren't always on the run. Unless the situation works itself out in another way."

Morgan turned to Emma, wondering if her daughter would be assigned a new name. And who would Morgan be this time? "You ready to take off?" she asked Emma. Her daughter had flown plenty of times, but always on a private plane.

"Yes." Emma smiled and nodded her head. "I'm ready."

Morgan slid her fingernail into the locket around her neck and eased it open. She stared for a long few seconds at Landon and Emma's picture inside, their faces pressed cheek to cheek. Deep down, she'd known all along that she would be with Landon.

She leaned her head back and closed her eyes again. Her heart cried for Kyle. But she'd done one thing differently this time, left a silver lining in an unbearable situation. Later, she'd tell Landon what she'd done, but for now, she planned to keep it to herself.

Kyle felt like he was in an entirely different episode of The Twilight Zone, wondering how he was going to recover from this. *Thank God for Lexie.* He squeezed her hand. "We should be landing in about an hour," he said.

They'd finally taken the boat to Kauai, then traveled to Honolulu, and went straight to the airport. Combining what little money they had left, they paid the fee to change Lexie's plane ticket and got her on the same flight as Kyle to LAX, then Houston. And a guy about Kyle's age had swapped seats with him on the second flight so he could sit next to Lexie. He didn't want to be away from her, even on the plane. She'd already said she never gave up on their love, that she knew he didn't write the email, and that she loved him more than ever before. But he knew Lexie well enough to know that something big was on her mind.

"Are you wondering if I ever thought about staying? I mean, if I thought about staying with Morgan and Emma?" Kyle held tightly to her hand, to assure her that he wouldn't have left her for them. But he planned to be honest too.

She laid her head on his shoulder, avoiding his eyes. In a whisper, she said, "It crossed my mind. She was your first love. And the mother of your child."

Kyle took a deep breath. "I thought about it." He felt her tense against his shoulder, and he nudged her until she locked eyes with him. "And there will always be a place in my heart for Morgan, and of course for Emma. But even when I tried to picture a life with them, Lexie... I couldn't picture my life without you."

Tears trickled down her cheeks. "I have something to tell you, and I don't want there to be anything between us."

He stopped breathing. "What?"

"I—I…" She squeezed her eyes closed as another round of tears trailed her cheeks.

"Lexie, what is it?" Kyle was desperate to know, but terrified too. He wasn't sure how much more he could handle.

"I can't have children." Lexie locked eyes with him. "So maybe you didn't make the right choice."

Kyle's heart pounded in his chest as he processed what she was saying.

She swiped at her eyes, trying to whisper as she spoke. "I'm sorry. I'm so sorry. I should have told you sooner. I was going to tell you before we got married, in case you wanted to back out. There's a long medical explanation, but I was in a car accident when I was younger, and it left me barren. My parents have been pushing me to tell you, and I was going to, and then I got scared, and…" She could barely breathe, she was crying so hard.

Kyle was glad it was dark and most passengers were sleeping. He searched for words of comfort, but he was speechless.

"You might have chosen to stay with them if you had known, and I'm so sorry."

"Lexie." He cupped her cheeks in his hands and kissed her on the mouth. "It wouldn't have mattered. I will always have a special place in my heart for Morgan, and I feel shattered about Emma." He paused, swallowing hard. "But I never want to be without you. I love you. Somehow, we're going to get through all this."

"But, what about having a family?" She buried her head against his shoulder again, but he eased her away and found her troubled gaze.

"We are each other's family, and God will set us on whatever path He deems right. As long as we walk the walk, live the right way, and hold steady to our faith, we're going to be fine."

Kyle's eyes widened. *Did I just say that?* The Lord was surely on the plane with them, feeding Kyle hope that all would be well, even though the pressure in his chest felt like an elephant was sitting on him. He was so stressed out, depressed, sad, happy, and thankful, all at the same time. It was no wonder his chest hurt. But then he remembered something.

"Awe, man. I forgot to take my pill this morning. Of all days." He unhooked his seatbelt and slipped quietly into the aisle, then opened the hatch above them. His small suitcase had barely fit, and he had to struggle to get it down.

"My suitcase," Lexie whispered from her seat.

"I figured it was. I grabbed the first one I found." He said a quick prayer that whoever had so neatly packed his things hadn't forgotten the pill bottle in the bathroom. And he'd been way too upset to even check before he'd left the hotel.

"Ah. Got it," he whispered to Lexie, handing her the bottle so he could stow his suitcase again. He eased back into his seat and twisted the lid. When he tipped the bottle, four pills fell into his palm—and a piece of paper. He took one capsule, put the other three back in the bottle, then unfolded a tiny note. His heart thudded wildly against his chest. There was only one person he knew who would leave him a message like this.

> *Kyle,*
>
> *This was the only way I knew to get word to you without anyone knowing. I promise you with all my heart, I will find a way for you to be in Emma's life. Once again, I'm sorry. This is my promise to you.*
>
> *Morgan*

Kyle was sure he had no tears left. His world had been rocked, spun, shattered, repaired, blessed, and rebuilt. He handed the note to Lexie and covered his face with one hand. After a few seconds, he opened his eyes and saw her smiling in the dimly lit plane.

"A message in a bottle," he whispered softly.

Lexie grabbed his hand, kissed the top of it, and smiled again. "What a whirlwind all of this has been, but I have to believe that everything is going to be okay. With his free hand, he touched the shell he'd strung and put around his neck, the one Emma had given him at the beach. "I'll be praying that Morgan keeps her promise."

"Me too." Kyle pulled Lexie's face to his, kissed her softly on the lips, and as she rested her head on his shoulder again, he begged God to keep Morgan and Emma safe, and for Emma to be healthy.

Then he prayed hard that Morgan would keep her promise. And that God would hear his prayer.

Epilogue

Fifteen years later…

Kyle kept his eyes looking forward, even though it was hard not to look at the beautiful bride walking next to him. His right arm intertwined with her left arm as they both took slow steps on shaky legs. He wasn't sure who was keeping who steady on their feet. Maybe they were holding each other up.

Guests rose to stand in the church where Kyle had attended worship as a child. Kyle praised God for allowing him to be a part of this fabulous journey. Even the priest had a smile stretched across his face as they approached the altar.

"Who gives this woman to be with this man?" Father Griggs asked.

Kyle glanced at Morgan, seated on the front row to their left. "Her mother and I." Then he smiled at Lexie, on the pew behind Morgan. "Along with her stepmother, Lexie."

Kyle's mother smiled broadly from where she was seated next to Morgan's parents. Somehow Patty had seemed to stay endlessly young, but Alex—the name he still used—had aged way past his years, and Kyle assumed the man's job might have played a big role in that.

When Kyle turned to Emma, he lifted her veil, and all of his memories from the past fifteen years bubbled to the surface in a euphoria of happiness. "You've never looked more beautiful," he whispered as he kissed her on the cheek. "I love you to the moon and back." A phrase that he now shared with Lexie and Emma.

She smiled. "I love you, too, Dad. To the moon and back." She glanced at Morgan, then back at Kyle. "I wish Landon was here," she said in a whisper.

"Me too. But he's smiling from heaven."

Emma's blue eyes twinkled as she took a deep breath.

Kyle's gaze drifted in Morgan's direction. He could still recall the conversation they'd had in Hawaii, when Morgan said, "What if he dies?"—in reference to Landon. A fear that came to pass much too early for her husband.

Landon been gone almost five years, but he'd been just as much a father to Emma as Kyle, maybe more. Lexie had told him once, that a child could never have too much love, and they'd all shared in Emma's life.

Kyle handed his daughter's hand to the man who would be responsible for her well-being from now on. Shane was a good man, and Kyle knew God had His hand on this, the same way He'd kept His hand on all of them over the years.

Morgan had kept her promise, but ultimately it had been Landon who closed the door on the case that had kept Morgan's family in danger. It should have been his time to enjoy a normal life, but colon cancer took him way too young.

Kyle returned to his seat. He glanced at Morgan and smiled. She had her arm around her twin thirteen-year-old boys, who looked more and more like Landon every year. Kyle turned to his left when one of his own boys poked him in the arm.

"What is it?" he asked Zackary, who was also celebrating his sixth birthday today.

"Emma looks pretty," he said, smiling with a big hole in his mouth where one of his teeth should be.

"Yes, she does." Kyle turned to Lexie and winked. Then he scanned their entire crew. All five of them. As it turned out, the doctors had been more than a little wrong about Lexie. Or maybe they'd been right, but God chose to gift them five precious miracles.

He tuned back into the ceremony, smiling, as Emma professed her love to Shane.

Be blessed in all that you do, Emma. As I am a blessed man to know you and love you.

Acknowledgments

To my family and friends, another big thank you for your continued support as I travel on this amazing journey. Special thanks to my fabulous husband, Patrick, for being patient and tolerant when I'm up against a deadline, especially when it's a 'fend for yourself' dinner night.

Audrey Wick, it's an honor to dedicate this novella to you, and I do so with much appreciation. A huge thanks for the time and level of professionalism you gave to this project. Not only were your revisions spot on, but it was also a joy to work with you. I value our friendship, and I'm your biggest cheerleader when it comes to your own writing. So write and prosper! ☺

To Reneé Bissmeyer, Diana Newcomer, and my mother—Pat Isley—thank you for your dedication to this novella. And Karla Hanns, thank you for jumping in at the last minute to help finalize the manuscript.

And, as always, Janet Murphy…you rock! Much appreciation for everything you do to keep me on an even keel, as marketing guru, research aide, assistant, voice of reason, and way too much to list here.

To Wiseman's Warriors—much thanks to all of you for continuing to promote Beth Wiseman books. I'm blessed to have such an amazing street team, and I hope we'll all be on this journey for many years.

If I've forgotten anyone (and it's happened), please know that it takes a team to publish a work of fiction that entertains and inspires. I hope I've done that with this project, and I'm deeply grateful to everyone involved.

To my heavenly Father. Thanks and praise for all that You are in my life and for blessing me beyond my wildest dreams.

About the Author

Beth Wiseman is the best-selling author of the Daughters of the Promise series and the Land of Canaan series. Having sold over 1.5 million books, her novels have held spots on the ECPA (Evangelical Christian Publishers Association) Bestseller List and the CBA (Christian Book Association) Bestseller List. She was the recipient of the prestigious Carol Award in 2011 and 2013.

She is a three-time winner of the Inspirational Readers Choice Award, and an INSPY Award winner. In 2013 she took home the coveted Holt Medallion. Her first book in the Land of Canaan series—*Seek Me With All Your Heart*—was selected as the 2011 Women of Faith Book of the Year. Beth and her husband are empty nesters enjoying country life in South Central Texas.

Other books by Beth Wiseman

The Daughters of the Promise series (Amish)
Plain Perfect   *Plain Paradise*
Plain Pursuit   *Plain Proposal*
Plain Promise   *Plain Peace*

Land of Canaan series (Amish)
Seek Me With All Your Heart
The Wonder of Your Love
His Love Endures Forever

Amish Secrets series
Her Brother's Keeper
Love Bears All Things

Women's Fiction
Need You Now
The House that Love Built
The Promise

Surf's Up Novellas
A Tide Worth Turning
Message In A Bottle

Visit www.bethwiseman.com for more information about Beth and her books. Visit Fans of Beth Wiseman on Facebook.

CPSIA information can be obtained
at www.ICGtesting.com
Printed in the USA
LVOW08s2138031116
511542LV00015B/466/P